REWIND

OTHER BOOKS AND AUDIO BOOKS
BY JEFF DOWNS:

Heaven's Shadow

REWIND

a novel

Jeff Downs

Covenant Communications, Inc.

Covenant®

Cover image © Getty Images/Digital Vision

Cover design copyrighted 2004 by Covenant Communications, Inc.

Published by Covenant Communications, Inc.
American Fork, Utah

Printed in Canada
First Printing: August 2004

10 09 08 07 06 05 04   10 9 8 7 6 5 4 3 2 1

ISBN 1-59156-605-3

ACKNOWLEDGMENTS

Once again I would like to thank those who helped make this book possible. Ernie Riedelbach—thank you for sharing so much. You and Sheri are truly an inspiration to many. Thank you to Trent Summers, Brian Stewart, Tom Mackay and Ila Litz for your technical expertise, and to Gay Rothwell and Val Sawicki for cheering me on once again.

To JoLynn Davis, thanks for the name, and all—and I mean all—of the cakes; Karen and John Smuin for reading and sharing in the stories I haven't published—you still have me shaking my head when I think back on it; Jeff Haroldsen for accepting all personal correspondence mistakenly sent his direction; and the Ballards for their input on the story—you inspired me to go forward with it in the beginning.

I'd like to express my appreciation to Shauna Humphreys, the managing editor at Covenant. Also thanks to Carrie McGhie, who made a difference in my life! If it hadn't been for your e-mail and sticky note, this book would never have seen the light of day.

Thanks to Angela Colvin and all of the staff at Covenant (and I mean everyone)—you are all truly masters of your craft. My gratitude also goes out to Rhea Buttars, Kathleen Killian, Jeff Vale, Elaine Davies, Landon Coburn, and the Barzee, Contor (especially Josh), and Eckman families for all of their kind words and support.

Also, thanks to Deoine Gunderson who taught me the value of sharing; Fred "The Hulkster" Harper (for the friendship as well as the beatings); Bill Litz, whom I am very proud of; my parents, Steve and Jan, for all they've done for me over the years; and finally to my wife Kara, who, when I mentioned doing this, went out, bought the paper, and told me I could do it.

No man, having put his hand to the plough, and looking back, is fit for the kingdom of God.

—*Luke 9:62*

PROLOGUE

"He made you look like an idiot, Scott," Chad said suddenly, breaking the silence that had prevailed since they'd left the conference room.

Scott stopped walking in the narrow hallway in front of his office and glared at his friend and longtime partner in sales. "You never beat around the bush, do you, Chad?" he asked harshly. "You club it dead center and field dress it on the spot."

Scott entered his cramped office and took a seat behind a somewhat-cluttered desk.

Chad dropped into one of the two artificial-leather chairs directly across from him. "In this case, that's because I think there's something you need to learn from me, Scott."

"Chad, he's a program director; it's understood that he's ignorant about these things."

"He's been with this radio station four months, Scott. He's only building credibility every day. And with this sluggish economy and clients bailing out on us left and right, he's going to do everything he can to pin the blame on us, regardless of what Wall Street has to say. You've got to prove to management that he's wrong, not just wait for them to figure it out on their own. Look at how many announcers they've already sent packing in their . . . 'quest for excellence.' Just who exactly do you think will be next, if revenues don't improve, and if we can't show a plan of action?"

As Chad cleared his throat, undoubtedly preparing for a second assault, or at the very least to answer his own question, Scott suddenly managed a weak smile, a wry thought crossing his mind. "He'll do anything to hold on to that Jaguar, right, Chad?"

"Do you think this is some kind of a joke?" Chad's voice was rising.

Scott shook his head, putting up his hands slightly in a conciliatory gesture. "Of course not, Chad. Of course it's no joke. Believe me. He's—"

"Then stop taking so many cheap shots, Scott! You have to convince them that we *are* giving one hundred percent."

Scott was losing patience. His own voice grew louder. "Look, Chad, I handle things in my own way, all right? Just relax. Give it a little time—"

"And you and I will be unemployed!" shouted Chad. "Don't you get it?" And with that his friend jumped to his feet, straightened his tie, and stormed through the open door.

Scott just sat there, loosening his own tie and unbuttoning his shirt collar. He wasn't surprised at Chad's theatrics; he'd seen them displayed countless times in the past. But, deep down, he knew the man was right. He *did* get it. He knew it better than anyone else. And yet what was he supposed to do about it? Their station had been bought by a huge media conglomerate, and a new program director, Sky Remington, had been sent to see to it that their money hadn't been wasted. *But this isn't Chicago,* thought Scott. *They're bound to figure that out soon, right?*

And there it was—doubt. Scott had always relied on his gut to steer him in the right direction. It was the one lesson Scott's dad had drilled into him as a kid. Now Sky, Chad, and even his father-in-law were questioning his tactics. But how did you explain decisions made from the gut? Despite the fact that deep in his heart Scott knew he was on the right track, Sky's relentless barrage was really beginning to chip away at Scott's resolve.

Maybe I don't know what I'm doing. Maybe I'm completely out of touch. Maybe . . . maybe Sky's right.

His eye caught the computer on his desk. And, for the umpteenth time, he found himself wishing he'd stuck with the computer hobby he and his dad had enjoyed when he was younger. In the computer world, Scott mused, you dealt primarily with machines—a bunch of numbers really. *You* were in control. Absent were the silly mind games and hoop jumping he was now being forced to endure.

The humorous thought of simply switching Sky off, or of having him reformatted, flitted through Scott's mind. But the reality of the situation was that he couldn't do either of those things. Scott had to either deal with him, or go on just putting up with him—to ride it out and wait for the pendulum to swing.

How would Dad have handled this? Scott found himself asking this question a lot lately. His dad, a simple mailman and the bishop of their ward, seemed to balance things so well. Scott remembered him as easygoing and fun loving. He could be stern when he needed to be. But that wasn't often; he found ways around it. If his dad had only lived longer, Scott mused, maybe he'd know how to better handle the problems he faced.

But then his parents had only had one child. *Now three—that pushes out a few more gray hairs.* Scott smiled at his own predicament. But was Scott really remembering things the way they had been? Years had gone by. Perhaps the rose-colored glasses of the past got even rosier as the years sped on.

He swiveled his chair and looked out the small window of his office just in time to catch Sky slipping into his new sleek silver Jaguar. *Probably a bonus for condescending to come here in the first place.* Even on a program director's salary, Scott doubted Sky could easily afford such a car on his own.

As Sky backed out, Scott caught the license plate: SKYSDLMT. *Sky's the limit*, he thought. *What does that mean, anyway?*

The phone on his desk unexpectedly jangled. He lifted the receiver. "Hello."

"Hi, honey. You don't sound so hot." At the sound of his wife's voice, his mood lightened, but not much.

"Oh, well . . . executive meeting this afternoon was rough, Kate."

"I take it they didn't appreciate Bob's pulling out of his contract."

"Now there's the understatement of the decade." Scott gave a small snort of chagrin.

"Want to talk about it?" Kate offered.

"Oh . . . Sky just pointed out to everyone that this is the third client that's bailed on us this month. He wants to know why I'm not pushing for litigation."

"Litigation?" Kate sounded taken aback. "Bob's just having a rough time with his business. He'll be back as soon as he can afford to advertise. Aren't you always telling me that you can't get blood out of a turnip?"

"*You* know that, hon, and *I* know that, but Mr. Jaguar is millimeters away from rebilling Bob at a higher rate for the months he's already used up. That alone might bury Bob."

"You're going to fight him on it, aren't you?"

"I'm working on it, Kate." Scott sighed. "It just feels like a lost cause."

"No, honey. Don't sell Bob out without a fight—"

"Kate," Scott interrupted, frustrated, "I don't know if there's a whole lot I can do about it."

Kate was silent for a few moments, then, quietly she said, "Just promise me you won't give up on him."

Scott lowered his own voice. "Of course I won't. It's just . . ." Scott couldn't finish the sentence; he knew it wasn't what she wanted to hear.

"Sky's just new, Scott. He doesn't understand how you do things around there yet. Remember, he's from the big city; he's a very small fish from a very big pond."

Scott laughed. "Trust me, hon, none of us here will *ever* be allowed to forget that he's from the big city. That I can assure you."

Several seconds passed in companionable silence before Scott decided to change the subject. "How's Justin?"

"I don't know. He was still kind of sullen when he got off the bus today."

Scott had exploded at his son the night before. He'd left home before seeing Justin that morning, and had felt bad about it all day. Apparently, so had Justin.

"I didn't mean to flip out, babe. But, dang it, the tent we have is good enough for what he needs it for."

"He was only asking if you'd seen the green one at Shopko."

Scott felt the heat rise once more in his face. "No, Kate. He *wanted* the green one at Shopko," he corrected. *Now there's a thought! I could hit Sky up for the tent. He could claim it as a charitable deduction. Then his high-priced accountant wouldn't have to leave that portion of the tax form blank for once. Or, better yet,* thought Scott, *maybe he'd let me come over and check the couch cushions. I bet I'd find enough for two green tents at—*

"You shouldn't have gotten angry, Scott. Swearing at him never—"

"I know, Kate. I know. I'll . . . I'll make it up to him."

Another long and awkward silence followed.

Scott's father never blew his stack the way Scott had.

Finally, in a tentative voice—a voice he'd noticed Kate using a lot lately—she said, "It's just that you've . . ."

"What, Kate?"

"It's been happening quite a bit lately, honey. Even the girls are—"

"Kate, look, I'm sorry, all right? I've been under a little stress here with the economy bottoming out and—"

"Scott, all I'm saying is you need to watch who you're taking your anger out on. That's all."

They'd had this conversation before. Each time Scott had committed himself to doing better. But, just as before . . .

"Hey, we can talk about this tonight when you get home. I called to remind you to pay the dentist before going to the mechanic tonight. The bill's a few weeks overdue. I've transferred some money into checking so we won't overdraft again. Those service charges are driving me . . ."

Scott's attention involuntarily drifted away from the conversation. He focused on the Jaguar's now-empty parking stall, and then his gaze shifted to the blue minivan parked in *his* stall; he had just replaced the transmission two months earlier. He suspected it now needed a new alternator—an alternator he couldn't really afford right now.

He thought of Sky once more. *Off to some party, no doubt. A few visiting friends from the entertainment industry showing their gratitude for making them look so good in middle America.* He had little doubt it would be a catered affair at what had to be a palatial home in the hills. *Perhaps they'd eat around the pool, or in the gardens.*

Scott gave in to his quickly souring mood.

Why is it I put in double the hours and yet . . . I'm older than he is, for crying out loud. The Jaguar, the trips, the money. The way Scott saw it, he'd be lucky to enjoy any one of the trips Sky had supposedly taken. And, to make matters worse, Sky did nothing but complain about where he'd been; Peru was too hot, Scotland too rainy, his Switzerland tour had lasted only seven days instead of ten (he'd apparently forgotten to add in travel time).

"Sweetheart?"

Kate's voice jerked Scott back into reality. "Huh?"

"You still there?"

"Yeah. Yeah, I'm still here. Sorry, I was just distracted for a minute."

"Look, hurry home, Scott, okay? Caitlin still has a bit of a fever, but what do you say we rent a video tonight? We still have some Double Fudge Delight ice cream in the freezer."

There's MY big party, Sky! thought Scott with an edge of bitterness, grimacing inwardly at what Sky might think if it. And to cap it all off, he knew he needed to help Glen, the elders quorum president, with two move-outs on Saturday. "Yeah, Kate. A video sounds good . . ."

Scott mumbled a good-bye and returned the phone to its base. For several minutes he just sat there staring at Sky's empty parking stall—his mind switching gears once again—wondering just what the man *would* do to maintain rule over his radio kingdom. The barrage of unjustified insults he'd hurled at Scott and Chad earlier that afternoon seemed to indicate that he might be willing to resort to anything. Sure, Sky was tough, charismatic when he wanted to be, and seemed to have a lot of outside connections, but he couldn't seem to connect with the mom-and-pop businesses in town. Scott acknowledged that they could be unreliable at times, but he knew that if you treated them well and you had enough of them, they made a good customer base. At least that's what Scott had always believed.

But Sky had been hired by the new station owners to take the third-rate station to "bigger and better heights." And individual addends apparently didn't work into Sky's equation for big-time success.

But the others at the station had to see his side of it, didn't they? After all, Bob had been with the station since its founding. Begin suing every client for breach of contract and it would just wipe the smaller businesses off the map. Of course, what choice did the others at the station really have? Even the station manager seemed intimidated by the "representative from on high."

Scott suddenly noticed how overcast the sky had become—droplets of rain randomly peppered his office window. The gray sky seemed to match his mood perfectly. *Great, a rainstorm*, he thought sarcastically. *That's what I wanted to drive home in—the perfect ending for a perfect day.* He stood and reached for his worn tan overcoat. *Why am I not surprised at rain?*

He met Chad at the elevator just as the twin stainless-steel doors opened. The silence was awkward as they made their way in. The doors had closed before Chad finally spoke. "Look, Scott. I'm sorry I blew up at you back there. I just don't like to see . . ." He hesitated, struggling, it seemed, to come up with the right words. Scott broke in.

"Chad, it's okay. Sky doesn't bother me. He's just a flashy young know-it-all. He'll come around to how things are done around here. Give it time. Really, it doesn't bother me."

Chad opened his mouth to reply but seemed to think better of it, opting for silence until the elevator sounded and the doors opened onto the station's small, quaint lobby. Then he sighed. "Okay, Scott. See you tomorrow."

Scott made his way to his van through the steady, icy rain. He pulled the collar of his now-slick overcoat tighter around his neck. "It doesn't bother me," he muttered, involuntarily recalling Sky Remington's final statement to the station manager. "Just maybe we need to get *someone* in here that *can* hold onto clients!" Scott's mission president in Guatemala, attempting to use reverse psychology in an effort to get Scott's zone out of a slump, had used a similar line on him years ago. It might have worked with someone who was truly slacking off. After his mission president dug a little deeper into the situation, though, he apologized for having tried the tactic. With his mission president, the remark had originated as a well-meaning catalyst, so to speak. But Scott knew that the same words coming out of Sky's mouth were meant as nothing more than a bold-faced threat.

Scott knew his speech about ignoring Sky probably sounded convincing enough to Chad. But deep inside, he knew his words were a cover-up—nothing more. Nearly everything about Sky *did* bother him—had for quite some time, and he was worried. Was staying the course really the answer? Scott just wasn't sure anymore.

He fumbled for his keys, the rain coming down now in sheets.

Scott had lied to Chad. Much worse, however, at some level he knew he was also lying to himself.

CHAPTER 1

Ordinarily a leisurely stroll through the quiet streets of his old neighborhood brought with it a feeling of peace and contentment, coupled with a longing for the carefree days of childhood—games of hide-and-seek, kick-the-can, and tag played late into the evening, the itching from playing in the grass and bushes lingering well into the night. Today, however, for reasons he couldn't quite put his finger on, Scott was finding the experience oddly disconcerting and out of place.

An open blue sky hung peacefully over the cracked, tree-lined sidewalk he was walking on. The gentle sound of rustling maple leaves overhead provided what seemed to be the only evidence of a slight spring breeze. It was neither too warm nor too cool. Everything was just right—a perfect day. *This* was what seemed to be bothering Scott the most. But before he could give the matter much thought, the distant sound of a school bell captured his attention.

It's been years since I walked by the old school, he thought to himself. *It'll be fun to see it again.*

He crossed the street and rounded a corner of tall hedges, noting that they were shorter than he remembered. He watched from a distance as a flood of elementary school children worked their way into the large yellow buses that lined the curb, nearly hiding the school building from view. A few kids got into the strange assortment of late-model cars parked along the street. Scott realized with amused satisfaction that the ones walking home in small clusters had chosen to walk on the opposite side of the street from him—a stranger.

If that's the final bell, then it must be later than I thought. Scott raised his left wrist to glance at his watch. *I forgot it again,* he realized.

I hate it when I do that. Without his watch, the day simply didn't feel right.

He continued walking toward the school, dodging the occasional sprinkler and grinning at a few penned dogs who barked loudly at his supposed invasion of their territory. By the time he had reached the school grounds, all of the buses and most of the cars had departed; the hint of diesel exhaust still lingered in the air. *I'm so glad I lived close enough to walk home when I was a kid,* he mused. *Buses are nothing but cattle carriers. They might be fine for a field trip. But every day? Forget it!*

A chain-link fence, oil-stained blacktop—faded parking lines still visible—and a half-burnt, dandelion-infested lawn announced he'd indeed reached the elementary school.

He stopped on the sidewalk directly in front of the sprawling single-level school and marveled at just how small it now appeared. Each of its buildings was linked to the others with overhead steel awnings which theoretically protected you against the occasional rainstorm. And each passageway his eye picked out brought back so many memories. He must have walked to the redbrick lunchroom a million times, and to the playground three times that number. As his eyes wandered over the outer buildings, he found himself remembering indelible events from his youth—monumental events they had seemed: the stumble and consequential denting of his Six-Million-Dollar-Man lunch box, the Halloween parades he'd marched in, the school plays he'd helped move sets for, the clump of bushes he'd hidden in so he wouldn't have to take the dreaded standardized test for that year. Scott smiled at this last memory. *Makeups—there was no escaping them.* Scott decided to explore behind the main building before going to the office. He wanted to see the old playground. He remembered hearing on some TV news show that the deadly monkey bars and the dreaded merry-go-rounds had been ripped out of schools across the country, and he wondered if the ones he remembered were still there. But most of all, he wanted to see the Swamp: a portable classroom located at the extreme end of the school grounds. It had often been used during years of overcrowding, and it was a room in which he had fond memories of the fifth and sixth grades.

It was a battered building, with large spots of rust eating through the off-white paint on the exterior walls. Both of his teachers had assured him that during an earthquake they were in the safest building in school since the walls had been designed to fall outward. It wasn't until several years later that Scott thought to wonder where the ceiling would go when that happened.

It surprised him that the old building was still here, seemingly unchanged after nearly twenty-four years, but it was somehow comforting. *I wonder if it still stinks inside?* Despite every one of its large windows being opened as often as possible, the smell of mildew and newly applied roofing tar had always seemed to fill the room— hence the building's affectionate nickname. Scott and his classmates had all just gotten used to it. Its flat roof had always leaked, and it now seemed a miracle to him that no one had died from exposure to some toxic mold.

He stood staring at the beige, rust-streaked building for some time, his eyes eventually drawn to the strangely colored construction-paper eggs hanging from inside its huge windows. He smiled. *I remember that project!* Scott had forgotten one could combine spray starch and tissue paper, then draw with drops of ink by blowing through a straw.

His brow furrowed with his next thought: *Surely Mrs. Call isn't still teaching.* The next moment he shrugged to himself. Truthfully, Scott had no idea how old she had been at the time. Perhaps she'd been quite young. After all, anyone over twenty years of age had seemed ancient to a ten-year-old boy.

Scott decided it wouldn't hurt to check. *Besides*, he thought, *it'd be kind of fun to visit with her again.* He found himself nervously tugging at the wrinkles in his simple white T-shirt and checking to see how bad his jeans were.

"Mr. Davis." That's what she used to call me, remembered Scott fondly. *"Mr. Scott Davis."* He now realized that she had probably thrown it out whimsically, but at the time he had thought it made him sound a bit more grown-up, causing him to hold his chin up just a little bit higher. It was something he had needed at that point in his life. *Who knows*, he thought with a smile, *maybe she'll be shocked to discover that the shortest kid in the fifth grade finally topped out at six foot two.*

Approaching the building, he reached for the doorknob, but it unexpectedly flew away from his hand and a dark-haired boy bolted past him at breakneck speed on his way out the door.

Scott smiled. He couldn't blame him. He, himself, had rarely hung around the building after the final bell.

He stepped through the open door and was immersed in memories as it slowly closed behind him. Textbooks, pencils, and the alphabet-and-number line above the chalkboard confirmed that this was a classroom. The size of the chairs and desks surprised him; they had always seemed so much bigger. But as his eyes scanned the room, he noticed that, in fact, the entire *room* seemed much smaller than he had remembered it.

Toward the front of the classroom he could see the top of a bobbing head—a child on his knees, struggling, it appeared, to clean out his desk.

Man, how Mrs. Call would ride me about that! he remembered. *If she knew what my desk at the radio station looked like she'd probably have a fit!*

Scott stood for several seconds, absorbing the smells of chalk, paste, and—sure enough—mildew. When he realized that Mrs. Call (or whoever the teacher was now) wasn't anywhere in the room, he decided he'd better carry on with his walk. But the moment his hand hit the doorknob, his curiosity got the better of him. *I've gotta know if she's still teaching. The colored-paper eggs are too much like hers for it to be anyone else.*

Scott turned his gaze to the front of the room and cleared his throat. "Excuse me."

The boy was obviously startled. He had clearly not realized that anyone was in the room with him. But when the young boy's head rose above the clutter of books and wadded paper on the desk in front of him, Scott's shock must have been a hundredfold that of the boy's. He felt his legs grow weak, the blood drain from his face. *It's . . . it's me!*

CHAPTER 2

"I didn't mean to! I . . . I swear I didn't!"

"Relax, ma'am! Just relax! Do you have a cell phone?"

"Well, yes. Yes, I do!"

"All right. Call for help and I'll see what I can do. And when you're done, there's a blanket in my rig—behind the seat. Grab it."

"I . . . I feel terrible! I honestly didn't—"

"Please! Make the call! There's no time for this! Hurry!"

* * *

"Wh—what's your name?" Scott formed this question with a great deal of confusion and some trepidation. He had recovered enough to conclude that his earlier question about Mrs. Call would surely remain relevant once the boy confirmed that his looks were just some surreal coincidence. All the same, Scott didn't know how it was possible for the boy to look so much like himself at that age.

The boy had clearly felt uncomfortable under Scott's bewildered gaze, and had gone back to cleaning his desk. Now he looked up with obvious reservation but answered in a quiet, subdued voice. Perhaps he hoped that giving the tall stranger his name would make him go away. "Scotty Davis." Then he went back to work.

Scott found himself reaching for the nearest desk in an attempt to steady himself once more. *What is this?* He squeezed his eyes shut, willing away what he'd just seen and heard. Scott leaned on the desk, muttering to himself. He rubbed his eyes with his hands. "This isn't real. It *can't* be!" he whispered. "I'm thirty-four years old, married, and have three children." But when he pulled his hands away from his eyes, the classroom was still there . . . and so was the boy.

I don't believe this! Scott stared at the young boy; he studied his clothes, his physique, everything about him. His dark brown hair was the right color, although in need of a haircut—or was that the style then? *I've forgotten about that sprinkle of freckles I had above my nose.* It was as if he were watching an old home movie, but able to interact with the image. He shook his head, trying to make sense of it all. Then it dawned on him: *He isn't real!* That *had* to be it. This was the most twisted joke anyone had ever played on him. He must be on some kind of reality television show he'd never heard of before. *Yes!* he thought, desperately turning his sudden hypothesis over and over in his mind. *That has to be it! There's just no way . . .*

He looked around the classroom suspiciously for any sign of a camera, a two-way mirror, or . . .

Nothing.

Real fear began rising to the surface of his mind.

The sound of crumpling paper brought Scott's head up. He glanced at his wrist futilely, as if knowing the exact time would help him make sense of all this. Absentmindedly he found his right hand moving to grip his bare wrist, to confirm by touch what his brain could not trust from his eyes alone.

But when he saw his hand, he froze. *His scar! Of course! That would be incontrovertible proof.*

With determination, Scott moved slowly toward the boy—Scotty—who appeared to be nearly finished with his cleaning. Scotty didn't seem to notice Scott's approach over the sound of his books being crammed into a newly created gap in the contents of his desk.

Bits of broken crayon and other odds and ends remained on the boy's desktop, and they stirred something in Scott that was more familiarity than actual memory. At the precise moment the boy reached up to grab his wooden ruler, Scott shot out his own hand and caught the opposite end of it. The boy instinctively tugged, but Scott held firm, lifting his own hand slightly and turning his wrist clockwise.

There it is! Between the first and second knuckle of the boy's index finger ran a scar, marking the spot where a pocketknife had closed on his finger in the fourth grade. "Scotty *Davis?*"

The expression on the boy's face immediately turned to pure panic. He gasped, let go of the ruler, and bolted for the door.

As the door swung slowly shut, Scott could only sit on the edge of a desk, stunned.

What in the world is going on here? He stood and again looked around the room. "Okay!" he yelled, "you can come out now! The joke is over. Ha, Ha! Nice job."

The room remained silent.

And now another disturbing thought came to mind. *But . . . nobody knew I was coming here. I didn't even know it until—*

"Don't you think you were a bit overbearing with the boy?"

Scott whirled around upon hearing the voice. Nobody was there.

His heart began racing once again. "All right," he called out, a strained smile developing on his face. "I said the joke's over. You can come out now."

"This is not a joke," replied the voice.

Scott quickly backed up, turning this way and that, desperately searching the room for the source of the deep and resonating voice. But it didn't seem to be coming from any single direction. It seemed as if the words were blanketing him from all sides.

"Relax, Scott," said the voice in a conciliatory tone. "I assure you, you're not losing your mind. Everything you see is just as it seems. And the boy you saw . . . *was* you."

Scott shouted, "Look! I don't know who y—"

"I had thought that showing you what was possible first," interrupted the voice regretfully, "would be the easiest way to convince you of what I am about to tell you, Scott. I admit I might have been wrong. I am not infallible. Perhaps fewer distractions would be helpful."

The classroom around him suddenly dimmed and then faded completely to black, Scott was caught off guard. His surroundings had seemed so real, so tangible. He spun around, looking for the desks, the chalkboard, the school—anything!

Everything had simply vanished.

Scott found himself standing in the middle of complete and total blackness. Nothing could be seen or heard anywhere around him. Nothing.

For nearly a full minute it was all Scott could do to catch his breath and calm down. He had so completely accepted the world around him, and to unexpectedly plunge into darkness was unfathomable and frightening. It was as if every one of his senses had simply been shut off.

Then Scott slowly lifted his hands and was surprised to discover that he could see them. A glance downward confirmed that *he* was visible in an environment seemingly void of light and substance.

But how can I see myself? he wondered. *Where's the light coming from?* He could see no sun, no fire, no lightbulb—nothing.

Cautiously, he crouched down and felt around with his hands. The blood drained from his face once more; he had honestly believed he was standing on a solid surface. Now, he realized that the nothingness did indeed completely surround him—even beneath his feet.

Panic began to rise up within him. Was he falling? Had he somehow entered a cave and was now plunging to his death? Scott put his hands to the sides of his head, trying to get a grip on himself. He couldn't be falling. He would hear and feel wind rushing by if he were.

"Hello!" he called out. He could hear his own voice clearly, though it was understandably shaky. It sounded odd to him, and then he realized that while there was no sound distortion, there was also no echo.

Scott cleared his throat, startling himself with the noise. "Can . . . can anyone . . . hear me?"

He swallowed, gaining a little more confidence. "Hello!" he called out more loudly. "Can anyone—"

"I can hear you, Scott," replied the mysterious voice. "I'm still here."

As shocked as Scott had initially been at hearing the voice in the classroom, he felt an odd sense of relief at its return.

"Where am I?" he asked.

"The first thing I'd really like you to do, Scott, is to relax. Everything's all right."

The absurdity of this statement brought a nervous chuckle from Scott. He straightened. "All right?" His courage was beginning to return. He held out his arms. "*This* is all right? I don't know where you come from, but for me," Scott again glanced all around him, irrationally hoping someone would flip a switch, "this is definitely not all right."

"I promise you, Scott, you're perfectly safe," the voice said reassuringly.

Scott chuckled again, still nervously. "Right." But his apprehension faded to curiosity. "Where am I, anyway?" he asked again. His bravado quickly crumbled into frustration. "Just what in the world is going on? Who are you?"

"I am your friend, Scott. You might call me your guardian angel, but I'd prefer just 'Guardian.'"

Scott gave a short bark of laughter and waited for more, but the voice did not continue.

"That's it? *That* is supposed to explain everything? How does that explain all of *this*?" Scott asked, flinging his arms out in an inclusive gesture.

The voice did not respond.

Scott looked down at his feet. He carefully raised a foot and then pressed down toward the blackness in front of him. It was solid.

Scott dropped to one knee and felt all around, stunned yet again to discover nothing but emptiness around and beneath him. He stood again, raised his foot, and tapped it against the space directly in front of him. Once more it met solid resistance at the same level as his other foot. It was as if every step he took landed on an unseen solid surface exactly reflecting the size and shape of his own foot.

He gathered courage and gave a tentative hop. Though his mind told him he might easily break through whatever was supporting him, he found that he did not; a floor existed, but only when he needed one. Cautiously he took a few steps. Pacing usually helped him concentrate, and after taking several steps he found his mind naturally returning to the situation at hand.

Scott paced for several seconds before voicing his one overriding thought: "This makes no sense! Do you hear me—whoever you are?"

He stopped walking, frustrated at not having a specific direction to address the enveloping voice. "You told me everything in that classroom was real," he challenged. "Now I find out it . . . it was nothing but an illusion."

At this the voice did respond. "It wasn't an illusion, Scott. I promise you that. What you saw *was* real."

"Come on," Scott replied skeptically. "The trees, buses, the school, all of that—including Scotty—was *real*?"

"That's exactly what I'm trying to tell you."

"And even though I can't see any of that right now, it's still real?"

"It is."

Scott blew out a breath he hadn't realized he'd been holding and threw up his hands. "Well now I *know* I'm nuts. If that's the best you can come up with—"

"Scott," began the voice again, with a soothing and calming air of patience, "was it *not* real? Couldn't you feel the light breeze, hear the dogs bark, smell the diesel fumes? Didn't you touch the ruler, and sit on the desks? Couldn't you feel the warmth of the sun on your face?"

The voice—Guardian—had him there, Scott realized. He had definitely experienced for himself all of the realities of that spring day. *Even the sound of the leaves,* he remembered.

Scott suddenly became aware of the fact that he was being lulled into accepting what he'd seen as real, when in actual reality he was standing in the middle of nothing. He couldn't possibly grasp how it was possible for the classroom and this all-encompassing darkness to exist at once. "Wait a minute. Just hold on *one* minute!"

"What is it, Scott?"

Scott brought his hand to his face, rubbing his eyes, and pinching the bridge of his nose. He was trying to put all of his confusion and frustration into words when a single thought suddenly demanded his attention—*Spring!*

He rolled the thought over in his mind. "It's not spring!" he concluded, his voice rising in volume with new confidence. He didn't know why he should suddenly feel so adamant about it, but he did. "It's *not* spring!"

Scott looked all about him, expecting some kind of a response, but there was nothing. Scott waited several more seconds for Guardian to respond, but when he appeared to have chosen not to, it confirmed his suspicion that he must have hit on something critical to his situation.

"It's *not* spring!" Scott repeated firmly, proud that he was now sure of *something*. "Did you hear me? It's not sp—"

The voice finally responded. "But, Scott, I never said that it was."

At this Scott gave a smile, satisfied he had recognized at least one inconsistency in what the voice had been trying to make him believe. He was silent for several seconds, thinking carefully over his one "fact."

A second thought eventually followed on the heels of the first. *Rain!* Scott excitedly verbalized it. "I . . . I remember cold rain! It's raining!" Of course at the moment it wasn't, but Scott was oddly certain it had been.

A long pause ensued while Scott desperately tried to put his thoughts together. "Fall . . ." he mumbled. "This is supposed to be fall!" He smiled the more he considered this, and eventually exclaimed, "Okay, whoever you are. I've got you. I couldn't have experienced a springtime stroll because it's really fall."

"That's exactly right, Scott," replied the voice. "It's fall."

Latching onto this one certainty, he abruptly challenged the voice. "All right then, *Guardian*, whoever you are. Enough is enough!"

"What do you mean?"

"Oh, come on. I've figured you out. None of this is *real*. You yourself admitted it's not spring but fall. Well, which is it? It can't be both."

"Scott, if you will listen to me, I promise you that—"

Scott ignored the voice, plowing toward the only conclusion he felt he could make that was based on any sort of logic. "Now I get it. I'm dreaming all of this. It's nothing but a dream—a very realistic one—but a dream nonetheless. That's the only thing that makes sense!"

"Scott, please take my word for it." The guardian seemed almost to plead with him. "This is not a dream."

Scott clenched his jaw, irritated at how easily his conclusion was being dismissed. "If all of this isn't a dream, then tell me, Guardian, what it *is!*"

"I was preparing to do just that, Scott. Please be patient with me. I only wanted to give you some time to get over the shock of your new surroundings."

Scott glared at the blackness surrounding him. "What surroundings?"

Scott thought he could detect amusement in the voice as his apparent guardian continued. "Scott, please listen carefully. This is important. You are being given an incredible opportunity. You might say it's the ultimate gift." The guardian paused as Scott struggled to comprehend the meaning behind his words.

Then, almost as if to get it over with, the voice finished in a rush, "You are being given the opportunity to correct three mistakes you feel you have made in your past."

CHAPTER 3

Scott laughed out loud. "I always knew I had an overactive imagination . . . but I can't *believe* this."

"Believe it, Scott. This is not a dream, and this is not a product of your imagination. As I was trying to show you before, what you are experiencing *is* real."

Scott grinned. "So you want me to believe that a genie has come to grant me three wishes?"

"I'm not a genie, Scott." The voice sounded amused again.

Scott's frustration spilled over again. "Then what are you?" he shouted. "You tell me I'm not dreaming, and yet the spring I experienced wasn't spring because it's really fall. I'm sorry, whoever you are, but what am I supposed to conclude here?"

"Scott, I realize all of this seems a bit strange, but please believe me when I tell you that it *is* real. You have truly been given the chance to change three mistakes in your past."

Scott stood silently for what seemed a long time, trying to think clearly. While he wanted to burst out laughing, his gut—his heart—oddly enough, was telling him he was hearing the truth. And yet he found the whole suggestion ridiculous.

"How—" he began, but the voice interrupted him, suddenly terse.

"Scott, you have been given the chance to change three mistakes you've made in the past. Will you accept this gift? Or should I leave now?"

Scott was still dumbfounded. What did the voice mean by, "Should I leave now?" Leave where? He smiled at the absurdity of such a statement. And if anything, it was Scott who should have been permitted to leave; he was the one standing in the middle of nothing.

A dream, he thought. That was the only explanation. All of this had to be a dream. If he even suggested the idea again, the voice would only deny it, but it had to be a dream. True, he couldn't ever remember being this alert and attentive to what was going on in a dream before. He'd had deep, vivid dreams in the past, but never had he been as—as self-aware in them as he was now. He did feel a bit confused, but his mind seemed clear. He was apparently capable of making decisions without his dream taking over as he remembered usually happening when he slept. Often, in his more vivid dreams, when he would begin to be aware of what was happening, he would either wake up or the dream would suddenly shift in setting, time, or scenery. Was that what was happening now?

Scott finally decided to humor what could only be his own subconscious. "Let me get this straight," he began. "You are going to allow me to go back in time and *change* mistakes I've made in my past?"

"Yes, Scott. Three of them. That's exactly what I'm saying. Though from the tone of your voice, I get the feeling you still doubt my words, and perhaps even my existence."

Scott threw up his hands. "What am I supposed to believe?"

"Precisely what I'm telling you."

Scott remained silent. He didn't want to start arguing with himself. If he started doing that, it would only be a hop, skip, and a jump to his first straightjacket fitting.

For several minutes he just stood in silence, hoping the voice— the guardian—would try to advance their conversation. Scott remembered hearing somewhere that dreams usually only lasted fifteen minutes on average. He could wait this out.

* * *

Scott was getting nervous. While he didn't have a watch, it felt like several hours had gone by. He was now sitting on the "floor" that had supported him automatically, even though he could feel with his hands that there was nothing under him. He kept waiting. He did not speak, and neither did the voice.

The time just kept passing and Scott slowly began to consider the concept that he actually might not be in a dream. He had no explanation for it, but it was now clear he wasn't going anywhere. Nothing changed. The enveloping blackness merely remained. After a while, his resolve began to wane very thin.

The voice had maintained its silence, but deep inside he could feel his heart telling him again that the voice was real, that he really was being given a gift.

"You're waiting for me, aren't you?" he finally said.

The voice immediately responded, its volume startling Scott after such a long silence. "I am."

Coming up with his own logical explanation for all of this had not done any good. He had nothing. Clearly he had little choice but to trust the mysterious voice. The longer he considered this, the more his mood began to lift.

Okay . . . He was supposedly being given the chance to go back and change three mistakes from the past. Why not? Dream or no dream, it was clear he wasn't going anywhere, so he might as well make the most of it.

"So, I can change three events in my life. Any events I choose?"

"Changing decisions might be a more accurate way of looking at it, Scott. You have the chance to correct what you feel are three wrong choices you have made—regrets, you might say."

Scott's joints felt stiff as he stood up. He jammed his hands into the pockets of his jeans and began to pace again—the earlier fear of the walking surface all but forgotten.

What if he could make changes in his past decisions? What if the past *could* be altered? Scott looked at both of these questions more seriously. He could continue sitting here doing nothing, possibly forever at the rate things seemed to be going, or he could . . . go along with the voice—try to change his life for the better. What did he really have to lose?

Scott decided he would do it. It didn't really matter how strange and bizarre the whole situation seemed to be. He cleared his throat. "Am I just supposed to tell you what decisions I want to change and . . . poof?"

Scott again thought he detected the hint of a smile in the guardian's tone. "I'm afraid it's not that simple. You let me know each decision you want changed, as well as *when* you want to approach your younger self to suggest the change."

"Suggest?"

"Yes, Scott. There is still the factor of agency to consider. You have free will to make your choices. However, while your younger self will in time become you, he is not yet you. By the same token, you cannot unilaterally change his behavior for him based on your experience, which he has not yet attained. What you can do is act as a guide, and persuade him to make a different choice than you made in your previous past. You will have the opportunity of meeting with your younger self, just as you did in the classroom. It will be up to you to convince your younger self to act differently. If you manage to persuade him, he will move forward in time, and the change you suggested will produce new consequences for those actions."

Scott remained silent, deciding, *Okay, I think I can do that.* He could think of several things he wished he had done differently. Finally, after much careful thought, he decided which three decisions would be the best to correct and when he could most easily correct them.

The guardian listened patiently without interrupting while Scott explained his choices. Only after he had completely explained himself did the voice speak once more. "Very well," was the response. "Shall we get started?"

"Anything's better than sitting around here," replied Scott with a smile. He sensed disapproval from the guardian at his levity, and he wiped the smile from his face. He set aside his lingering doubts, giving the guardian his undivided attention. He might as well take this as seriously as the voice seemed to.

"Lead the way, Guardian," Scott amended in a more somber tone. "Lead the way."

CHAPTER 4

Scott found himself back in the classroom he'd just left, though a few of the bulletin boards seemed different somehow. He seemed to be alone, but he spoke into the silence.

"Uh, hello?"

"I'm here." The guardian was still with him.

"I don't get it. This isn't where I expected to be. Wasn't I just here?"

"Not exactly. It's been a month since you 'introduced' yourself to Scotty. I had a feeling you'd start with this age, and so I thought I'd help Scotty get over the shock of seeing you before you got started."

That sounded reasonable to Scott. "But I don't get it. Where is—"

"Look in your desk, Scott," interrupted the guardian. "In the back. There's something I think you'll want to see."

Scott just stood there feeling lost. "But I don't see Scotty or Jer—"

The guardian interrupted again, calmly but insistently. "Your desk, Scott. Look in the very back of your desk. Hurry. You don't have much time."

Scott briefly wondered why the guardian didn't try tactics other than persuasion to convince him to look in the desk, but then realized that was the formula he was to follow with Scotty. Suddenly Scott smiled as he caught himself giving the voice more power than it really had; it was a manifestation of his own subconscious after all! *Just play along with it, Scott,* he reminded himself. *Just play along.*

Scott walked to his desk, cautiously dropped to one knee, and reached slowly inside. His hand found something—smooth, yet bumpy. He pulled it from the desk. Scott took a deep breath. He hadn't been prepared for the emotion this small object was triggering. "It's the clay heart I made."

The guardian remained silent and Scott continued.

"I . . . I was saving it for Mother's Day."

"I thought you might enjoy seeing it again." The guardian sounded pleased with himself. Scott *had* been excited. He'd been *very* excited—there was no denying that. But when they'd broken it . . . Scott lifted his head suddenly, and he addressed the voice without hesitation. "Today *is* that day, isn't it?"

"Isn't this what you wanted?"

"I just thought I'd meet him as soon—"

"I didn't want to drop him in your lap, Scott. Are you sure you haven't changed your mind? This is the event you want to change?"

"Are you kidding? Seeing this heart again only makes me more sure. I want to do this," Scott said confidently.

A sound that could only have been a sigh came from the guardian. "Then you must hurry. Soon Scotty will be facing his choice. School ended only ten minutes ago. Scotty's a third of the way home by now. Here's your chance at creating your first change, Scott. You'd better get moving if you don't want to miss it."

Quickly replacing the clay heart, Scott almost flew out the class-room door. After several steps he stopped in front of the office, marveling at how real this all felt. *Maybe there* is *time,* he thought, shaking his head in confusion, suddenly throwing himself into the moment.

Scott began sprinting down a path he knew would intercept the boy's. *What if there IS time?*

CHAPTER 5

As he ran, cutting through front yards and side streets, Scott's thoughts were focused intently on what he would need to do to prevent his first major "mistake." He pried from his reluctant memory every old haunt and shortcut he could think of, until he'd finally spied the tall cluster of juniper bushes he'd been looking for.

Reaching them, he crouched into the small open space within the cluster, just as he had innumerable times as a child during games of chase, tag, and hide-and-seek. Of course he couldn't remember being this winded as a child, and for a few seconds he worked at catching his breath as well as collecting his thoughts. Only then did he realize how ridiculous he must have looked, sprinting as he had. He hoped he hadn't been spotted by another adult—or even a child for that matter. Still breathing hard, he peered around the tall bushes, looking up and down the sidewalk that ran in front of the large, unkempt shrubs. He couldn't see anyone in either direction.

Scott then poked his head back out the opening through which he had entered. The dark brick home was a good fifteen feet behind him, and as far as he could tell, nobody was home. That was good. The last thing he needed was for someone to come charging out of the house demanding to know why a grown man was hiding in their bushes. What would he say? What *could* he say? Should he say anything? He chided himself for worrying about things that were irrelevant, since this was, he reminded himself, only a dream.

Throwing all of this aside, Scott returned his focus to the task at hand. If he really could prevent what was about to occur, he was willing to try. It was either this or return to nothingness—and whatever that nothing was, it got boring fast. *Hang in there,* he told himself. *Just go with it. What have you got to lose?*

Sitting there, marveling at how real everything looked, felt, and smelled, he became distracted, and didn't notice himself beginning to stand. The prickly, barblike shrub brought him out of his reverie. He winced and returned to his haunches, pulling the dry prickles from his hair and collar. He crouched low, and again looked down the sidewalk to his right. Scotty should soon be coming around the corner at the far end of the street, and Scott sat back, waiting for him.

He almost hadn't needed to bother coming up with this plan. For years he'd pondered what he could have done differently that day. Now all he had to do was—

He heard a whistle.

That's MY whistle, he thought dizzily, wiping what he considered to be very realistic sweat from his forehead. He forced the lingering doubts from his head. *Go with it,* he kept telling himself. If this wasn't real, it didn't matter, but if it was, he was only going to get one shot at this.

Scott knew what he had to do.

He watched as Scotty walked past and up the sidewalk. He didn't want to scare him, as he had before with the ruler. His first thought had simply been to grab him. After all, he was only going to be talking to himself . . . his younger self. But if in fact he had been given the chance to change the past, he would have to be careful around those with whom he interacted. Real people or not; he had to assume they were unpredictable. He wouldn't have any more control over their actions than he had with the people he worked with, or his wife and children. He grinned to himself at that thought.

Slowly he worked his way out of the bushes, brushing prickly burs from his hair and clothing. He took a few steps forward before calling out to Scotty.

Scotty's whistling ceased. He turned around quickly.

Scott immediately held up his hands. "Scotty, I'd like to talk to you a minute if I could."

The boy's eyes squinted slightly as he tried to place this strange man. When his eyes widened a few moments later, Scott knew he had been recognized from their encounter a month earlier. He would have to gain the boy's confidence fast before he panicked and decided to run. He kept his hands up and remained perfectly still. "Scotty, I'm sorry about . . . last month. I promise you, all I want to do is talk to you. I'm not going to move an inch from this spot. If I do, I'll understand if you run. Just believe me, Scotty, I'm only here to help."

The boy's shoulders seemed to relax a bit. "What do you want?"

At this Scott smiled. Where was he supposed to begin? How much did his subconscious expect of him?

"Scotty," he began, deciding the direct approach was probably best, "I'm you."

"What?" Clearly Scotty was confused. Alarm also began to show on his face.

Scott tried again. "You are me, and . . . I am you." Scott wondered why he was suddenly having such a hard time communicating. He was disgusted with himself for not being able to find the right words. Shouldn't he be able to talk even more clearly with himself?

The boy had clearly misunderstood his intentions. "Look, mister. If you need help, you probably ought to go see the police or something."

This is stupid! Scott thought. *You'd think my subconscious would cut me a little slack here.* He sighed, digging deeper for patience.

"Scotty, I'm you, only older," he tried to clarify.

The boy looked confused. He turned to walk away, but Scott had an idea. "Wait. I don't blame you for not believing me. I can prove it."

Scotty turned once more to face him, curiosity in his expression.

Scott licked his lips. "Listen. You like a girl in your class. Her name is Laura. Laura Neville. At night you work on ways of getting up the courage to speak to her."

Scotty's eyes widened. He had the boy's attention at least. "Your favorite idea is to get in an accident right in front of her house," Scott continued. "She'd come out and care for you until help arrived. She'd be brokenhearted and cry over you. Scotty, how would anybody else in the world know that?"

"I don't know." Suspicion and fear warred on his face. "Maybe—"

Scott interrupted him, hoping to reassure him with more proof. "Scotty, that day at recess, when you snuck into the classroom and looked at her clay figurine, it fell apart in your hands. You panicked and threw it in the school dumpster, hoping no one would ever find out. As far as I know, no one did."

The boy opened his mouth, but nothing came out. After a moment he closed it again.

Scott continued. "Scotty, listen to me. I know this sounds impossible. But believe me, I . . . I'm *you*."

After a moment of staring, the boy found his voice. "You're . . . me? I mean, I'm you?"

Scott couldn't help smiling. "It appears so, no matter how you ask it."

"But why didn't you just tell me this in the beginning? You just grabbed my ruler—"

Scott held out his own hand and pointed at his scarred index finger. "I was checking for this."

The boy's eyes narrowed in suspicion, but he took a few steps forward. His eyes widened once more at seeing the white line on Scott's finger. He held up his own small hand; aside from the difference in scale, the shape of each hand and the placement of the scar were a perfect match.

"But what's happening?" Scotty asked faintly. "Why—"

Scott suddenly remembered the guardian's warning; he had little time for discussion about a subject he couldn't even get an explanation for himself.

"Scotty, listen . . ." His voice trailed off as, despite himself, he too wondered why this strange dream felt so real. He shook his head, tried to focus, and began again. "Scotty, can you trust me?"

"I . . . I don't know. I—"

"Scotty, there's no time! You're going to have to. I promise I only want to help you. You've got to do something I've regretted you *not* doing for years now."

The boy still appeared wary, but Scott did have his attention. He took a breath. "When you round the next corner, you're going to run into Jerry and his friends."

The boy's body stiffened. Scott understood and remembered his fear; the bully had done nothing but taunt and hurt him for years. At times it had seemed as though there wasn't any place he could go without running into Jerry. But Scott was surprised at just how *much* fear he could actually see in the boy. *And they say childhood is carefree,* he thought regretfully, clearing his throat and beginning again. "He's going to make fun of you . . . and hit you."

The boy stood there, looking at him. He didn't say anything, but Scott noticed how his eyes flicked from side to side, and how he turned to check behind him.

"I know you're probably thinking about taking Fourth Street now. But, Scotty, I want you to do something else."

In the next few minutes, Scotty made several different arguments about what he was and wasn't willing to do. But after much pleading, lecturing, and reassuring, Scott hoped he had managed to persuade the young boy to follow his advice. What had seemed to finally convince Scotty was when Scott brought up what would happen to the clay heart he had made for his mother if he didn't.

A still-bewildered Scotty finally shook Scott's proffered hand, turned, and continued up the street. The moment he turned the corner, Scott started after him. He needed to watch—to make sure events unfolded the way he hoped they would.

He brushed away a few remaining burs from the bush and considered how proud he was of his younger self. Little Scotty was demonstrating a great deal of courage right now—more than *he* had shown at the time. After all, Scotty now actually *knew* what he was about to face, yet he was still walking toward it. And he had agreed to see it through.

Would he?

CHAPTER 6

On rounding the corner himself, Scott felt a thrill of shock at the sight not thirty feet ahead of him. Scotty was walking right up to the trio of bullies that Scott had promised would be waiting for him.

This street was a busy one, and Scott took a seat on a bus-stop bench at the corner. He couldn't hear anything from this distance, especially over the sound of passing cars, but he glanced to his right every few seconds, anxious to see if his younger self would follow through with what needed to be done.

Jerry, decked out in his customary worn Levi's and black Led Zeppelin T-shirt, was standing in the lead, straddling his battered black-and-gold Mongoose bike, with two of his friends flanking him on either side, also on BMX bikes—though not nearly as battered as Jerry's. Scotty, as he approached, would be subjected to a barrage of taunts and teasing. He'd take it silently for a while, and eventually Jerry would wipe a hand through his shaggy blond mane, get off his bike, walk over to Scott, and attempt to intimidate him with his size.

Scott wished he could give Scotty the several additional feet in height he now enjoyed. Jerry, even with his clenched jaw and piercing eyes, didn't look nearly as intimidating as he'd remembered, now that Scott had grown up.

Scott glanced again over his right shoulder, just in time to see Jerry doing exactly what he had predicted—no, had *known* would happen.

The taunts would continue with Jerry's two friends looking on, laughing, until Scotty would come up with a smart-aleck comment of his own. Then Jerry would hit him. But he wouldn't aim for the body, as he'd always done in the past. Today Scotty would experience his first direct punch to the face. But today he would also learn that Jerry's punches didn't hurt as much as he had thought they would—for he'd soon take two more rights and a left.

Scott glanced over just in time to see Jerry's first punch. He winced at its impact, but was proud to see his younger self standing firm. His eyes now remained riveted on the scene, watching it play out precisely the way he remembered it.

Jerry's two friends hung back, apparently stunned, while the punching sequence played itself out. Scott studied their facial expressions carefully. *They* were his real targets—his true concern.

The two rights and the left followed. And then what Jerry hadn't expected—Scott watched Scotty taunt Jerry some more, and he got the distinct impression that Scotty was smiling. *He's realized it's true,* thought Scott. *What he feared most wasn't nearly as bad as he'd imagined. And he sees the doubt in Jerry's eyes!*

And then history began to change. Abruptly Scotty pivoted on his right foot and bolted through the nearest yard. Just as Scott had hoped, Jerry scrambled to get back on his bike and race after his Scotty to finish what he had started. If fear to a bully was like blood in the water to a shark, then a victim running scared was like chopped fish.

Divide and conquer; that was Scott's plan. One boy going against three would be too much for him to handle. He was sure that if Scotty could break them up and then stand toe-to-toe alone with Jerry, and do what needed to be done just as the other two caught up, his problem would be solved—the mistake corrected.

Just before turning to make a sprint of his own, Scott spied the car—the '74 Dodge Dart he'd been expecting. It was driving slowly past him, its driver looking this way and that—searching.

Scott's eyes darted to where the boys had been. *Scotty didn't see her!* he thought with relief. Taking off at a dead run, Scott cut a diagonal path through several unfenced backyards, completely absorbed in the moment. He *had* to get there in time to see it!

CHAPTER 7

Bicycle motocross racing was an obsession with young people everywhere when Scott had been a kid. His hometown was no exception. Behind a 7-Eleven convenience store, several kids had converted a vacant business lot into a mini BMX course of their own. Miniature sweepers, berms, and drop-offs made up the perfect arena for these "rookies." Scott knew that Jerry spent a lot of time there, and that made the location ideal. Not only might Jerry feel overconfident there, but the string of barbed wire surrounding the field seemed the ideal stall tactic against Jerry's friends; Scott was betting Jerry would simply throw his bike over the wire in his pursuit of Scotty, since he obviously didn't care about the shape of his bike, while his friends would make the time to take a less damaging route.

Cutting through a final set of hedges, Scott, nearly out of breath, approached the busy street, found an opening, and jogged to the 7-Eleven on the other side. Rounding the side of the building, he saw Jerry tossing his bike over the barbed wire, just as he'd hoped he would. Scotty darted behind the only steep drop-off on the track. Scott looked behind him and could just make out Jerry's two friends halfheartedly working their way up the street. He congratulated himself on pegging their reaction—after all, it had been Jerry that Scotty had laughed at, not them.

Not wanting to miss any of the action, Scott looked back around the corner just in time to see Jerry get back on his bike and pedal in Scotty's direction. Scott had guessed Jerry would probably stall by showing off for a while until his friends arrived, and so he wasn't at all surprised when Jerry tackled one speed jump, profanity and taunts pouring from his mouth as he banked around one of the many berms and worked his way slowly toward Scotty.

Here he comes, thought Scott. *Just wait till he reaches you. Wait.* Scott was confident that the last thing Jerry would be expecting was for Scotty to come out swinging. More than likely he was expecting Scotty to run again—run until he made it to the safety of his front yard.

Turning his head, Scott saw Jerry's friends finally making it across the street, heading toward Jerry and Scotty. His head darted back toward Jerry, who was now approaching the last berm leading to the drop-off Scotty had chosen to wait under. *He'll show off clear to the end.* It would be only seconds now.

He turned again to check on Jerry's friends. They had to be there when everything went wild. They *had* to be! And while his eyes easily found the two boys, laughing at having spotted Jerry, his eyes were immediately drawn to the small Dodge Dart also making its way down the street. *No!* moaned Scott. *Not yet! Not here!*

He turned his eyes back just in time to catch Jerry taking on the drop-off with a jump that swung his bike sideways in the air 360 degrees. Scott might have been able to predict a move like that from a blowhard like Jerry, but what he hadn't counted on was the thin layer of mud at the base of the drop-off where Jerry landed. The kids building the track hadn't focused on drainage. Jerry was now finding out just how dangerous a track could be without the necessary drain pipe.

It wasn't a bad crash. Chances were he'd biffed it a dozen times like that in the past. But this time would be different. For as Jerry slowly stood, cussing and struggling to untangle himself from the bike, Scotty came in for the attack, just as Scott had told him to. A reverse punch to Jerry's solar plexus knocked the wind out of him, and a follow-up right cross to the face knocked Jerry to the ground, just as Scott had known it would.

He's doing it! Scott thought in wonder. *He's remaining in control—not letting the adrenaline take over!*

Scott confirmed with a quick twist of his head that Jerry's friends had arrived just in time to see precisely what Scott had wanted them to see.

Both boys stopped their bikes, stunned. Smiling, Scott glanced once more at Scotty and Jerry. His smile quickly disappeared. Jerry was on the ground, and Scotty was still pummeling him with his fists. As Scott watched, Scotty got to his feet, but he wasn't walking away . . .

Wait! thought Scott, shocked. *Kicking Jerry when he was down was never a part of the plan.* He started toward the two, but froze in his tracks at the sight of the Dodge Dart quickly crossing lanes to pull alongside the dirt field.

"Run!" shouted Scott.

The kicking continued.

"Run, Scotty!" he shouted even more loudly.

The second call finally seemed to register, and Scotty's head came up, his eyes locking with Scott's, his face beet red, eyes watering. He took several deep breaths and wiped at the sweat on his forehead before nodding to Scott and turning to run.

Did he see the car? wondered Scott. *No. He couldn't have—it's just pulling up.*

Predictably, Jerry's friends were hightailing it in the opposite direction, afraid of being blamed for what had just happened—what they'd stood by and *watched* happen.

The sound of the Dart's door closing brought Scott's gaze back to Jerry . . . huddled on the ground . . . crying.

Scott was surprised; never in his life had he seen Jerry cry.

Jerry's nose was bleeding profusely and he was holding his left side with one hand.

Scott slowly shook his head, smiling in wonderment. *He did it! He actually did it!* Now completely absorbed in everything he was seeing, Scott was genuinely pleased. *I actually taught the kid a lesson!* he thought to himself.

"Are you happy with how everything's turned out here, Scott?" It was the voice again.

Scott jumped slightly, but recovered quickly. He almost felt surprised at how accepting he was of the guardian now.

Scott answered, "Even I must have forgotten just how much hurt and humiliation—how much rage and anger—I must have had in me. I admit I didn't expect it to come boiling out like that, but—" Scott straightened his shoulders and continued, a little defensively, his own voice unmistakably filled with relief. "You have no idea how much Jerry's friends tortured me through junior high and high school. They had to see I wouldn't stand for anything like that. *This* is what I should have done that day—sent a clear message with little room for doubt." Granted, he had only planned on two punches to deliver that message, but . . .

Scott spied Scotty cutting across the street a block away, undoubtedly making his way home. His sense of relief extended to Scotty as well. *He's got to be feeling like a million dollars!* After all, he'd just defeated his own Goliath.

"I may not know what you went through in junior high and high school, Scott," the guardian said, "but now, neither will he."

Scott frowned, confused by the guardian's attitude, but then his attention was drawn to Jerry's mother. She had worked her way through the barbed-wire fence and was kneeling by her son.

She was crying—crying hard and gulping for air.

Scott watched as Jerry's mother helped her son to his feet, brushing dust and mud from his clothes, pulling his reluctant form into her arms.

Scott wanted to look away. He didn't want to feel anything more than pride at what his younger self had just accomplished. But when her tear-filled eyes unexpectedly locked with his own, he couldn't help feeling, despite the victory, a sudden, unwelcome pang of guilt.

CHAPTER 8

"Showing Jerry and his friends I had the courage to stand up for myself *was* the right thing to do," Scott was saying. They'd returned to the black nothingness, and he was pacing. "If I had learned to truly stand up for myself early in life—"

"What about Jerry's mother?" interrupted the guardian.

Again, Scott felt a twinge of guilt at remembering the look in her eyes. He stopped walking. "Well, I admit I feel bad for her. But . . . she'll get over it. Like I said before, you have no idea what they put me through."

Scott suddenly felt the need to explain further. "See, what really happened that day was that I lost it too soon, and I just came out swinging. The adrenaline was pumping through me and I could barely see straight. None of my punches made contact—they were all too wild." He grinned. "But I still remember the look on Jerry's face. I'd scared him when I didn't turn to run." Scott paused, his grin disappearing. "Then, the day after the fight, I found that clay heart I had made for my mother. It was broken into several pieces. And guess whose faces I saw looking through the classroom window when I discovered it? And who kept mimicking my wild swings every day at recess for what seemed like weeks?" Scott's voice had risen in pitch. He stopped and swallowed, looking around as if daring the guardian to respond.

"Jerry's two friends?" the guardian asked obligingly.

"Exactly! I never finished the fight in their eyes. I swung wildly . . . and accomplished nothing. If I hadn't seen his mother when I did . . . if I had just stuck to it like Scotty . . ."

Scott caught himself, paused for a moment, and began chuckling. *What am I saying?* he thought. *I'm talking about it as if it really happened, and yet I can't bring myself to admit that Scotty becomes me without having made that mistake* . . . He shook his head. He may not have been able to think of an explanation for what he was experiencing, but he still just couldn't believe it was real. These changes couldn't be real . . . even though everything around him *felt* so real. And here he was defending these nonexistent changes to the equally nonexistent guardian.

"What is it, Scott?"

Scott shook his head and cleared his throat. He knew it would be pointless to bring up his doubts, although he knew his skepticism was obvious from the way he'd been talking with the guardian. Besides, he'd already made up his mind he would continue to see this through. Truthfully, he was starting to enjoy it. *What's it hurting to play along?* he told himself again before answering.

"Nothing, Guardian. Everything's fine." Scott then fell silent as he again began pacing in the dark nothingness.

"What would you like to do next?" the guardian asked.

Scott stopped and placed his hands behind his back. "What else? Let's go make the second change, of course."

"That's it? Are you sure you don't want to ask me any questions? Don't you need more information, perhaps, before you decide exactly when or where to make the change?" the guardian sounded concerned.

Scott only smiled confidently. "Why would I need more information about my own life? It's you that obviously needs more information than I've given you, because apparently I wasn't very specific about the place last time."

"That's true." The hint of a smile was back in the guardian's voice.

"So," began Scott, "if you don't mind, I'd like to be a bit more specific this time." Then he added with exaggerated courtesy, "If there's no objection."

"Of course not," the guardian said with mock stiffness. Scott was gratified that the voice had loosened up enough to engage in a bit of light banter. "You only gave me an approximate age—a few years older. So just where is it you would like to meet Scotty this time?"

Scott paused as if considering, but he had already decided. "It was a Saturday. A Saturday morning." Scott then gave the guardian an exact address, just to be sure.

"I wish I could give you the exact date, but . . . there was a rocket I built, years ago. The thing stood four feet tall, painted silver with a thin black stripe. It was a three-stage rocket—three engines! Took me a good two weeks to build. That thing went up like a dream, but I lost it. It just went up too high. In fact, I seem to recall finding only the fins from the first stage." He looked up from his reverie. "I want to visit myself on the day of that launch," he said firmly.

"But does your next change have something to do with a rocket?"

"No. No, it doesn't. The truth is I just wouldn't mind seeing it again before talking to Scotty." Scott realized he was beginning to enjoy re-experiencing his memories in such vivid detail. "Consider it a two-for-one wish," he said with a bit of a grin. "Costing you nothing, of course. If it's allowed."

"Of course, Scott. If that Saturday is when you'd like to visit, then that Saturday it shall be."

Scott had folded his arms and was about to respond, but found himself suddenly standing in the middle of the large high-school soccer field he'd often visited in his youth.

His arms remained tightly folded as he simply stood for a moment to absorb all of the detail: the clear blue sky overhead, the smell of the fresh-cut grass beneath his feet, the peaceful quality of the Saturdays of his youth.

Squatting to the ground, he brushed his hand over the grass, pulling up a few blades and rolling them between his thumb and forefinger. "It's so real!" he marveled.

"It is real, Scott," countered the guardian.

"I . . . I know. It's just . . ." Scott shook his head, shrugging off the urge to argue, though all his common sense, reasoning, and logic told him he was justified in his continued skepticism.

He stood again, tossing the blades of grass into the air. "So. Where am I?"

"You're where you always launched your rockets," the guardian answered promptly.

Scott rolled his eyes. "I know that," he said disgustedly, looking around, squinting against the day's bright sunlight. "What I mean is, where is my younger self—Scotty?"

"He isn't here."

"But . . ." Scott was confused, but was secretly wondering if this was the point at which he'd lose control of events as he always did—even in his most realistic dreams. He finally continued. "Look, I know you couldn't have misunderstood me this time. I told you specifically that I wanted to meet myself when I was a few years older, the day I launched—"

"And this is that day and the spot that *you* launched it from," the guardian interrupted.

Again Scott looked around him. Even the track surrounding the soccer field was empty. The only person Scott could see, other than himself, was someone he took to be the school's janitor, struggling with the grass catcher on his riding lawn mower some distance away. "Then where is Scotty?" Scott finally asked in exasperation.

"Scotty doesn't build rockets," the guardian responded matter-of-factly.

"Sure I did. Lots of them. From the Mosquito to Big Bertha, I've tackled them all."

"Not anymore, Scott."

Scott simply stood there in stunned confusion, his eyes drawn to a passing car. He watched it idly, not really seeing it. "Are you saying . . . that just because I beat up Jerry, I don't fly rockets now?"

"Precisely."

"Well, if he's not here," Scott vented some of his frustration in irritation toward the guardian, "then how am I supposed to talk to Scotty about the next change?"

"I'm afraid you're going to have to go where he is."

Scott snorted and rolled his eyes again. "Fine. And just where am I right now, if I'm not here?"

"About a mile and a half from here—at the junior high."

Scott waited through a long pause. Finally, he shrugged. "Well?"

"Well, what?" the guardian asked innocently.

"Aren't you going to take me there?"

"You told me you wanted to come here. I followed your precise instructions on bringing you to this time and place. What you do now is up to you." A short silence followed. "You do have legs," the guardian pointed out.

Scott shook his head in disgust. Wishing he knew which direction to glare, he made his way toward the opening in the chain-link fence.

CHAPTER 9

As it turned out, the mile and a half went by rather quickly. Scott reflected that as a boy he had taken many of these yards, streets, and cul-de-sacs for granted; they were his extended backyard and playground—nothing more. The older he got, however, the more magical these places had become in his memory. They had been, he realized, places where imagination had prevailed and where the worries of the real world weren't as important as knowing a good shortcut through so-and-so's yard for the next game of tag.

Now, through adult eyes, he was amazed to discover just how normal everything appeared. There were more trees and mature shrubbery in this area, perhaps, but, for the most part, it was identical to the small suburb where he now lived. So why didn't *his* neighborhood seem as magical today?

The answer seemed obvious—he was an adult now. He simply had more important, pressing things to worry about . . .

Suddenly Scott stopped walking. *Pressing things to worry about?* he wondered. *Why does that—*

"Is something wrong, Scott?"

Scott jumped, startled at the sudden interruption, the next moment feeling sheepish. *You'd think I'd be getting used to that by now.*

"I was just thinking," he muttered, and continued walking again.

He decided it *had* definitely been a treat to see so many older cars in one place. One just ahead caught his eye. In an attempt to make conversation, Scott commented, "Now that, Guardian, is a thing of beauty." He gestured at the 1971 Chevrolet Camaro RS Z/28 parked alongside the curb. It bore all the features he would have expected: it was black with white striping over the hood, and had a tall spoiler in the back, high-back seats, and polished chrome rims. "That is what a Camaro is *supposed* to look like!"

"What do you mean, Scott?" the guardian asked.

"I mean, nowadays all cars look the same." He smiled, remembering. "As kids, my friends and I would sit on the curb and race each other to guess the correct make and year of each oncoming car. I was pretty good at it, too. With today's cars, you can't tell the difference between a Lexus and a Cadillac; they all look the same—no unique style."

"I see," the guardian replied. But Scott wasn't finished yet.

"I remember coming home from the airport with Mom after my mission. There I was, marveling at all of the makes and models I *hadn't* seen in Guatemala, and then a Pontiac minivan passed us on the driver's side. Sloped windshield, massive taillights on the back—it looked like a space shuttle! They all did." He shook his head, continuing to walk toward the junior high he could now make out a few blocks ahead of him. "Kids would be lucky to identify the make these days, let alone the model."

He noticed the nearly empty parking lot first. "So, Guardian, just where am I supposed to be, given it's a Saturday?"

"It's just around back, Scott. Head for the bleachers near the football field."

Football field? Maybe I mow the school's lawns now, he thought with a grin.

Scott approached from behind the wooden stand of the visiting team's bleachers, but there was no one cutting the grass on the field. Instead, a large group of football players clearly practiced on the field.

"All right, Guardian. I'm here."

"Take a look at yourself," the guardian prompted.

Scott was confused. He looked all around, even up in the bleachers themselves. "I don't see me—*him*—anywhere."

"The playing field, Scott."

Scott walked around the end of the bleachers to get a better look at the players on the field.

Just then one of the coaches blew a whistle that brought all of the players into a circle at the 50-yard line. Scott couldn't hear what was being said, but it was obvious they were wrapping up their practice for the day, and soon afterward they were dismissed. Most players immediately removed their helmets and ran for their sports bags—some helping others out of their shoulder pads, others packing up their helmets and cleats and choosing to walk home before changing completely.

Two of the players began walking toward the bleachers, and the boy on the right caught Scott's eye. "That's . . . me."

"It is."

"But I never liked sports as a kid. I . . ."

"Built model rockets?" the guardian finished helpfully.

Scott ignored the remark, his attention focused solely on his younger self. He was amazed at how confident he looked, how he even carried himself differently than he remembered. But it *was* him.

"Well, Scott. What are you waiting for? It's time to make your second change."

Scott didn't respond. He was still staring at the football player.

"Scott?"

"What? Oh, yeah. It's just—" Scott smiled. "Look at me! It's incredible. All of this happened because of my first change?"

"That's correct, Scott."

Scott could only shake his head. How often had he wanted to appear *this* confident in junior high? It had been such an awkward period in his life—a constant struggle trying to "fit in." But now he looked . . . solid.

"You're going to miss your opportunity," the guardian reminded him.

Pulling himself together, Scott cleared his throat. "Okay, all right." He cupped his hands together and called, "Hey, Scotty!"

The two boys had started around the far end of the bleachers and didn't seem to hear. He tried again, louder. "Hey, Scotty Davis!"

Both of the boys' heads rose.

Scott motioned Scotty closer. "Can I talk with you a second?"

Scotty gave a slight nod and turned and said something to his friend—someone Scott didn't recognize—who shrugged and continued on without him. Scotty started toward Scott.

The closer Scotty came, however, the slower his pace became, until eventually he came to a complete stop. He simply stood there, eyes wide, mouth slightly open. He brought his hand away from his shoulder, slowly lowering his bulky sports bag and shoulder pads to the ground.

Scott belatedly realized just how shocking this might be to Scotty. He walked carefully toward him until only a few feet separated them. Scotty didn't move an inch, nor did his expression change in the slightest. Instinctively Scott sought to reassure him. "Scotty, it's okay. Do you remember me?"

After several seconds Scotty finally answered the question. "It's you!" he whispered, involuntarily backing up a few steps.

Scott slowly closed the distance, trying to calm the young man. "Don't run, Scott. I'm not here to hurt you. Don't you remember who I am?"

Scotty hesitated, studying Scott with a tentative interest. Eventually he was able to find his voice. "I've been . . . telling myself . . . that you couldn't have been . . . real."

Scott sympathized with the naked surprise on the boy's face. "Uh, well, I am, Scotty," he said awkwardly.

"But, you haven't changed at all. Aren't you wearing the same clothes? How—"

"Like I told you before, I really don't know how to explain this." He paused. "Look, let's get this over with, what do you say?"

"What are you talking about?"

Scott waved the young man over to sit with him on the bleachers.

Seated, Scott decided to break the ice with something positive. "You look great, Scotty. You really do. Bigger than I ever was at your age."

Scott could tell that some of the shock was slowly beginning to wear off. "Thanks. Um, look, thanks for . . . for what you did a few years back."

Years! thought Scott. *I guess it has been years for him.* "That's all right. Did I call it right?"

"You sure did. Jerry and his friends haven't bugged me since."

"I didn't think they would." He considered asking what had happened to Jerry, feeling again a touch of guilt over the intensity with which Scotty had delivered his blows, but decided it'd be a waste of time. "Do you still go by 'Scotty,' by the way?"

"Some of my friends still call me that," Scotty admitted. "I guess you can."

They sat in silence for several seconds.

"Oh. Mom liked the heart," Scotty offered suddenly.

This comment caught Scott completely off guard. Until now he'd only considered how his own past actions had affected *him*. At the mention of his mother, he began feeling uncomfortable. He *had* wanted to give the small gift to her so badly. Now . . . he had? He felt slightly dizzy, wondering if her life had changed as much as his obviously had.

"So, what now?" asked the boy with a smile.

Scott smiled back, realizing he must have been staring off into space. Before he had time to second-guess himself, he began to speak.

First, he assured Scotty that just as he'd had success with the last piece of advice Scott had given him, he'd have as much success this time if he followed through with Scott's next suggestion.

Scotty studied Scott's face with intense interest as he delivered his speech, hanging on Scott's every word.

Scott urged Scotty to get out more, to not retreat so much into hobbies that closed him up to the world around him—to open up his circle of friends. He emphasized that Scotty needed to enjoy life, to not take everything so seriously.

Scotty admitted that he'd already gotten to know quite a few of the guys on the football team. Scott applauded this and assured him it was a step in the right direction. Scott concluded, summing up his concern in one statement, "I just don't want to see you stuck with only a handful of friends like I had."

Scotty nodded slowly, looking thoughtfully at the ground. "Is that everything?"

"It is time to go now, Scott," the guardian interposed gently.

Scott didn't jump at the sudden voice. He was beginning to grow accustomed to having the guardian around, though it was now clear that only he could hear the voice.

"Yeah. That's it, Scotty, for now. I've got to go."

Scotty stood cautiously, frowning uncertainly at these words. He turned to leave, but then stopped. "You are real, aren't you . . . Scott?"

Faced with the sincerity of the young man's question, Scott found himself believing his own response. "Yes, Scotty. I am." He then offered his hand and the two shook, his younger self a bit wide-eyed at the touch.

"Will I ever see you again?"

Scott gave the young boy a quick grin. "In a few years," he confirmed.

Scotty nodded slowly at this and turned to leave once more, walking away and looking over his shoulder a few times until he passed from Scott's view.

Scott remained rooted in place, watching the bewildered boy as he headed home. *He's confused*, he thought. *But hopefully he'll follow my advice.*

"Satisfied?" asked the guardian finally.

"You know, I believe I am," Scott began, and he meant it. "I mean, I still haven't come to grips with this whole thing but . . . yes . . . I've enjoyed this." He gestured toward the young man now disappearing around a distant corner. "I mean, just look at him. He's learned to stick up for himself. And soon he'll be widening my . . . his . . . circle of friends. Why shouldn't I be satisfied?"

"Then you're ready to go?" the guardian asked.

Scott turned, scanning the playing field. There was something that didn't feel *quite* right, but . . .

"Sure, let's go," he answered finally. "Why don't you take me directly to my next change?" He held up his hands reassuringly. "Don't worry. I'll trust your discretion this time," he said wryly.

"Very well." The scenery began to fade.

Me and football? thought Scott, still amazed. *Who would have imagined that?*

CHAPTER 10

Scott had little doubt it was his last thought that had triggered what the guardian had decided to serve him up next. Even so, he was a bit perplexed to find himself standing not in a secluded section of his former high school, or somewhere else he could have another quiet conversation with Scotty, but in the topmost corner of the packed bleachers of his high school's football field.

The bleachers were filled with former classmates, sprinkled here and there with parents, all finishing at that instant their part in the "wave." As Scott seated himself with the rest of the crowd, he was amazed at all of the faces he recognized. Of course, a few were givens: several of the cheerleaders, the class president, and a few of the more sports-savvy students in the school—he remembered the faces, but not the names. It had simply been too long. Besides, he had rarely ever attended a football game with his friends, so it was doubtful he'd run into anyone here that he had really been familiar with.

The pep band at the opposite end of the bleachers started in with a number Scott was sure had been designed to inspire the team. Though, with a few of the clarinets squawking unexpectedly and the spattering of trumpets all seeming hesitant to hit a solid note, he questioned what positive impact they could be having on the team— or even the fans, for that matter.

It was early evening, and the football field was awash in the glaring artificial illumination of the overhead field lights. It was neither too hot nor too cold. Again, the weather bothered him; the voice had admitted after all that it was fall—a cold and rainy fall. And even if he was traveling in time, he doubted the weather had been this perfect his whole life.

To his right, a huge portable stereo, tuned to a local station, was blaring out a commercial for a mattress retailer. He couldn't tell who it belonged to, but everyone seemed content to leave it on.

At that moment several football players, half in pale blue, the other half in red, broke from the crowds around their respective sidelines and took their positions on the field. To his right, the radio seemed to respond to this cue, picking up with a man calling the play-by-play for what was apparently the local radio station. "Okay, sports fans, after that time-out, the Vikings are at the line of scrimmage; the tight end on the right, the split end is out to the left—the narrow side of the field. Quarterback, Crockett, up behind the center. The fullback is Bishop and the tailback's Sampson."

"Guardian? What's going on here?" Scott asked, completely confused.

No response from the guardian. None of the nearby spectators turned to see who he was talking to, either, leading Scott to wonder if he was actually here, and whether he could interact with anybody in this scene. He certainly didn't see himself anywhere.

"The center snaps the ball to Crockett. Crockett turns left, hands the ball off to Sampson. Sampson's going left between the tackle and the tight end, and gets a great block upfield from his wide receiver. He's heading toward the 20-yard line. He's now to the 15 . . . to the 10-yard line . . . 5 . . . and *in* for the touchdown!"

The stands erupted with cheers. Chants of support followed, led in part by the cheerleading squad below, with the band—caught off guard—struggling to throw in its two cents as well. Scott located the scoreboard: 33 to 7—Vikings out in front.

The Vikings set up to kick the extra point, the announcer keeping up a patter of names and statistics to fill the time.

"Guardian?" Scott tried again.

Still no response.

"Holding will be the quarterback, Crockett, for Sanchez. Sanchez is a transfer out of Mexico . . . has come to play football now for the Vikings . . . has that soccer-style kick."

Scott couldn't help smiling as Sanchez took the field. He remembered him from several of his classes. Sanchez had really struggled during his first two years of high school. Fortunately, while English was new to him, sports hadn't been. When fellow students saw what he was capable of on the soccer, baseball, and football fields, they didn't seem to mind digging deeper for patience, and gave the guy the slack he'd needed socially. Eventually Sanchez, with his huge smile, had become fairly popular, and once he got a fairly good handle on the language, seemed to do well academically his senior year.

"The kick is up . . . and good," bellowed the announcer. "The Vikings now lead 34 to 7 over the Rebels."

The bleachers exploded once again with cheers. Across from the Vikings crowd, the visiting team's bleachers were nearly silent in comparison.

"And we'll be back with the kickoff from the Vikings, right after these messages from our sponsors."

"Sanchez is a good kid, isn't he, Scott?"

The voice startled him again.

"So now you're talking?" Scott asked, a little peeved.

"You didn't want me to interrupt the play, did you?"

Scott smiled at the hint of humor in the guardian's voice. "No, I suppose not," he replied. No one in the crowd seemed to notice him or hear the voice. And despite the crowded, chaotic atmosphere, he realized he could hear the voice as clearly as he had when they'd been alone. "So, tell me, Guardian. Just how am I supposed to have a nice one-on-one chat with myself here?"

"Oh, there's no way you could chat right now. Scotty is much too busy concentrating on the game."

Scott reflexively scanned the crowd once more . . . and then his eyes slowly dropped to the Viking bench: *Davis*. There was *his* name on the back of one of the pale blue jerseys. "You've got to be kidding me."

"Of course not, Scott," responded the guardian. "See?"

At that moment Scotty pulled off his helmet to accept a paper cup of water or Gatorade from a much younger-looking boy. Then he turned and gave someone in the bleachers a thumbs up. Scott followed Scotty's gaze to the other end of the bleachers and found his mother. "Mom?" he murmured to himself.

She sat with a smile on her face, yet it was clear from her posture that she didn't feel too comfortable sandwiched between a set of parents and the flute section of the band. Scott was amazed at how young she looked.

The blaring ad was finally over, and the announcer, who Scott decided was probably sitting in the press box to his distant right, once again sprang to life. There were about four minutes and thirty seconds left in the third quarter. Mecham, tailback for the Rebels, caught the kick and ran until he was pushed out of bounds at the 40-yard line.

But Scott missed it. His eyes were boring into the back of the young Scotty Davis sitting on the bench. *I'm in a football game,* he thought, stunned.

I'm in a football *game!*

Scott returned his gaze to the game just as the ball was snapped to the Rebels' quarterback and quickly handed off to the tailback—who only made it three yards before the noseguard collapsed on him. An incomplete passing play followed.

"For the Rebel offense it's third and seven—Rebels need that first down, and a lot of points, in order to get back into this game against the Vikings."

Scott sat up straighter. "Okay, I get it. You've brought me here so I can watch Scotty make the winning play, right? It'll be down to the wire—a real nail-biter."

"Scott, haven't you noticed the scoreboard?" The voice was patient, but Scott detected a trace of mild sarcasm.

"Yeah, but there's still a lot of game left. Do I catch the winning play with only a second to spare in the fourth quarter?" he asked eagerly.

"Just how common do you think a play like that is?"

Scott didn't bother to answer, his attention once again drawn to the game and a third down passing play for the Rebels.

The Viking fans erupted with cheers as a Rebel receiver, having been flipped the ball, was taken down one yard shy of the first down—the team was now forced to punt back to the Vikings.

"It's a high kick," continued the announcer, "floating just a bit. Sampson waits for it at the Vikings' 30-yard line—taken at the 30 . . . goes right. But he's taken down at the 35-yard line."

The band erupted into yet another chaotic number as the crowd dutifully clapped along. "So it's first and ten now for the Vikings. They continue to lead 34 to 7 over the Rebels and they'll go on offense once again late in the third quarter. Vikings have called a time-out. We'll be back after these messages."

"Now I play, right?"

"What makes you say that?"

"Because you seem to cut to the chase. I don't think you'd bring me out here to watch the whole fourth quarter before something happens. So, whatever it is you want me to see is coming up any minute now, right?"

"I think we're beginning to understand each other, Scott," the guardian said wryly.

Scott didn't reply as, just then, Scotty ran onto the field. *I knew it!* thought Scott with some satisfaction. He leaned toward the radio.

". . . Vikings out of the huddle now. They have Davis, tight end, set up on the left side, slotback and wide receiver set up on the right side, and Crockett at quarterback. Vikings have a first down at their own 35-yard line, and they still lead 34 to 7."

Scott quickly glanced over at his mother, checking to see if she was watching. She was, though Scott couldn't detect a lot of excitement. *She's probably been to so many games, she's seen it all,* he decided.

The announcer continued. "McDonald gets the snap from center, goes straight back to pass. He's looking downfield . . . looking deep for his wide receiver. Looking deep . . . he can't find him. He's covered, well covered, down deep. Looks to his outlet valve . . . and gets the pass out to Davis."

Scott jumped to his feet with the rest of the fans.

"Davis, the tight end, has the ball at the 47 . . . ooh, gets hit at the 50-yard line, knocks over a linebacker at the 50 and is on his way now—has open field from the 50 down to the 40 . . . down to the 30 . . ."

The announcer's voice was becoming more and more excited as the crowd went wild.

"He's hit again by a linebacker for the Rebels . . . but gets away—spins away!—and he's headed for the goal line! Down to the 20 . . . the 15 . . . the 10-yard line—two safeties are waiting for him at the goal line!"

Scott swallowed hard, unconsciously holding his breath.

"He muscles his way between two linebackers . . . over the top of the safeties . . . and . . . *in* for the touchdown! Vikings are now up 40 to 7, making a rout out of our game as the Vikings come back up now to the line of scrimmage, setting up for the extra-point-after attempt."

"That was incredible," mumbled Scott. He had returned to his seat along with the rest of the fans. "I can't believe he just . . . how in the world did I—"

"It's all in where your focus is, Scott," the guardian interrupted. "If football and working out become your primary focus, then of course you'll succeed at them."

Scott glanced over at his mother. She was clapping, though he'd expected more enthusiasm.

"Did you enjoy that, Scott?"

"Yeah, I did. But when am I supposed to talk to him?" asked Scott, gesturing toward the field. "You made me walk a mile and a half last time. I trusted you this time. Don't tell me I've got to camp out here all night in order to—"

"No, Scott. The game was my idea. I didn't think you'd mind seeing this before having your final conversation tomorrow. Consider it a kind of two-for-one wish—costing you nothing, of course," the guardian explained smoothly.

Scott grinned. "You know, Guardian, I think you're right. I think we are beginning to understand each other. Okay. Let's go."

The world around Scott began to swirl as he saw Sanchez kick the ball. Scott didn't get to find out if the kick was good or not, but knowing Sanchez, Scott was sure he'd nailed it.

CHAPTER 11

"Will you be by the same time tomorrow?"
"I think so."
"It's a shame. And Christmas right around the corner."
"We've done all we can do."
"I know. It's . . . it's just such a shame."

* * *

Pizza, burgers, fries, Pepsi, thought Scott. *And America wonders why diabetes and heart disease are on the rise.*

Still, he had to admit, *it does look good!*

Scott eyed the popular fast-food line in his high-school cafeteria, comparing it to the regular lunch line to his right, serving up the more traditional—and more affordable—servings of green beans and macaroni casserole. The smells and sounds around him inundated his mind with memories. How many times had he and his friends sat around a lunch table planning an after-school adventure, talking about nothing in particular, or cramming for an upcoming test? More times than he could even remember, he decided.

As his eyes swept the room, he was again surprised to recognize so many faces. It was almost as if he'd never left. The majority of their names were lost to him, but they all looked like they were exactly where they belonged, doing what he'd always remembered them doing.

He moved out from behind a stack of chairs to get a better look at the scene before him.

I can't believe all the corduroy, Swatches, and big hair! he thought with a grin. *Did we really wear all that?*

He spotted, at the far end of the cafeteria, a table of girls that had always caught his eye at lunch. They looked just as they should with feathered hair, puffy sweaters, and dark, tight jeans. They each picked at their salads as they always had, giggling and laughing, seemingly unaware of admirers watching from afar—though, with a more mature perspective, it was now obvious they had known *exactly* what they were doing. How could he have missed such a transparent act, even as a kid?

Scott walked along the outer edge of the long lunch tables, catching snatches of varied conversations. Topics ranged from boys to girls, some poor teacher obviously just doing his job, and, of course, the incredible row over the night before—undoubtedly the same game Scott had witnessed. He got a kick out of how dramatic the students were with each other in describing it. Each play was painted with rapid, short sentences and a flurry of hand gestures, exaggerating each play to border on the supernatural. But then, who could blame them? It had been a great game.

His third and final change had seemed to require a more mature Scotty, so he had asked to visit himself during his senior year of high school. After having witnessed how well Scotty had done on the field, he was even more confident that Scotty could handle his next suggestion.

At the other end of the room, he saw four boys rise from their table and head for the cafeteria doors. There he was, one of the four. And to Scott's surprise, he was wearing a blue and black letterman's jacket, to boot.

He followed the four from behind, keeping an eye on them as they made their way toward the glass-and-steel doors. Occasionally, Scotty and the others would stop to tease or flirt with girls at the ends of lunch tables; Scott marveled at his confidence, how he was so comfortable with his emotions—he didn't seem the least bit inhibited.

Scott couldn't help feeling some pride at this. After all, his suggested changes had produced it, right? It was definitely an improvement from the shy, uncomfortable soul he *had* been.

As he walked from the cafeteria, Scott sank his hands into the pockets of his jeans. It wasn't exactly cold outside, but the slight wind did carry a hint of fall and was a touch cooler than he'd experienced thus far. He followed the four boys through the open quad—lined with benches and trees just as he remembered it.

Though it was cloudy and cool, several groups of students were enjoying the fresh air, taking a break from the stuffy hallways and classrooms. Many were simply talking, but there was loud laughter from one group; whatever joke had just been told, Scott didn't think it could have been *that* funny! He chalked it up to adolescent hormones and continued on.

Eventually Scotty broke off from his three companions and walked over to a bench where two girls were sitting. Scott couldn't hear what was said, but suddenly felt embarrassed at what took place. Scotty made room for himself on the bench by squeezing between the two girls. He then began nuzzling the ear of the girl on his right. She appeared uncomfortable—even a bit scared. When she tried to get up, he pulled her back into place. Her friend stood up and raised her voice, telling him to back off. But Scotty simply laughed and continued to press his obviously unwelcome advance.

Scott quickened his pace and called out to him.

"Scotty!" Then louder, "Hey—Davis!"

The young man and both girls immediately looked up, undoubtedly expecting a teacher. Scotty's expression was definitely annoyed. The girls, on the other hand, were clearly relieved.

Scott saw recognition dawn fairly quickly on the young man's face. A broad smile emerged. Scotty stood and released the young girl's hand, tossing it aside. "Well, well, well. If it isn't my *big* brother." He turned to the girls. "Wait here. I'll be right back." The moment he started toward Scott, however, both girls took off in the opposite direction.

As his younger self approached, Scott couldn't help commenting on what he'd just witnessed. "A little pushy, weren't you?"

Scotty grinned. "Ah, they want me," he said dismissively. "They just don't know it yet."

Scott was put off for an instant at his arrogance. But the sheer confidence that radiated from his younger self eventually rekindled his smile. How many times had he longed for exactly what he was seeing in Scotty now? *He knows who he is!* Scott thought. *And he's comfortable with it—completely comfortable.*

It didn't come as a complete surprise, then, when Scotty took the initiative. "Come on, I know a place where we can talk." He headed in the direction of the football field. After a few steps, he stopped. "You did want to talk with me in private, didn't you?"

Scott shook his head to clear his dazzlement, giving the now-more-mature Scotty his full attention. "What was that?"

"You want to talk with me in private, right? I've waited several years for this," he added, the girls now clearly forgotten. Scotty was apparently completely familiar with the drill now.

"Oh, yes." Scott nodded. "Yes, I do. Someplace private."

Scotty nodded and resumed walking forward. Scott, once again focused, followed along behind. "So, what brings you here this time?" Scotty asked over his shoulder.

Scott had begun to wish he had on more than just a flimsy T-shirt, and dug his hands deeper into his pockets before answering. "Well, it's about your future."

Scotty snorted. "I could have guessed *that* much."

The strong, determined tone of Scotty's voice rattled him. "You've done well since we first met, haven't you?"

"How do you mean?"

Scott's pace slowed. *That's right,* he thought. *He doesn't know the difference. He's had nothing to compare his life with! Well, that could be remedied.*

Taking a deep breath, Scott proceeded to describe, as they walked, what *he'd* experienced in junior high and high school, leading up to and including his eventual move into radio. Scotty listened intently, shaking his head every once in a while—laughing outright more than once.

"Man, if I'd had to look forward to that every day, I think I might have killed myself!" he laughed, managing a "no offense" soon after.

Seeing the bright future the young man now enjoyed, Scott couldn't help smiling himself. He appreciated how humorous everything he described must seem. Still, it had been his life. He reminded himself to keep this crazy experience moving forward, to see it through. He was nearly finished anyway, right?

They reached the field and took a seat on the nearest bench—on the visitor's side. From here Scott could clearly see the press box from which so much excitement had been broadcast earlier. A few cups, soda cans, and wadded napkins littered the stands. He was surprised at how empty they seemed now—like a skeleton without the life-giving flesh and muscle.

After Scotty's laughter had subsided, Scott finally asked him, "So, have you given any thought about what you want to do with your life?"

All traces of amusement faded from Scotty's face. "What do you mean?" It was the first time in this conversation that he had sounded uncertain.

"Well, I mean, have you thought about the kind of career you want?"

"Now you're sounding like Mom." Scotty frowned and looked out over the field.

"Well, it *is* your senior year, Scotty. You shouldn't be completely surprised that people are asking about things like this."

Scotty kicked at a clump of brown grass near his foot, and Scott could see the uncertainty in his eyes. "Well, I . . . I was hoping for a football scholarship of some kind. But, I don't know. I'm not exactly the best out there," he said, indicating the field with his hand.

"Are you kidding, Scotty? You were fantastic out there last night."

"You saw the game?" His face lit up as he turned back toward Scott.

"Just the end of the third quarter. You were amazing."

Scotty flashed a wide grin. "I *was*, wasn't I?"

So, thought Scott, *there is still a bit of self-doubt buried down there.* He wouldn't have guessed it was there at all. Perhaps everyone had some of that, he mused. Even the people you'd never expect it from.

"A scholarship, you said?"

"Yeah. Scouts will be coming through soon. This school gets its share."

Scott nodded with satisfaction, realizing just how well this would go with his next change. "Mom will appreciate that, you know. Any kind of scholarship you can get would be great, but . . . what'll you major in?"

"Who knows?" Scotty said glumly.

Scott smiled triumphantly. "That's exactly what I thought you'd say. That's *one* thing we still have in common. I hadn't made up my mind at your age either. And I'm telling you, I lost a lot of precious time. But listen, because I'm about to change all that. How would you like a career path that can't lose?"

"Anything sounds better than what you just described. A radio station? Selling air? Ha! That'll be the day."

Scott ignored the jab, ebullient at how he was sure his next change would play itself out. "Well, listen carefully, then, because what I'm about to tell you could make you a very wealthy man."

Scotty sat up a little straighter. "You've got my attention, dude."

Dude? I'd almost forgotten how often we said that. Scott forced himself back on track. "Now, you already know a little about computers—"

"Yeah. They're for geeks," Scotty put in.

"*You* have one," countered Scott.

"I do not!" Scotty protested indignantly. He opened his jacket. "Do you see a pocket protector, dude? Does it look like I wear glasses?"

"But Dad—"

"Oh, that. It's been in the garage for years."

Scott was taken aback. Obviously, his earlier suggestions had resulted in a few changes, but he hadn't expected computers to completely disappear from his life. If he didn't know much about them, would his idea still work? He decided to press on—it was too late to change his mind now. This was the only change he could make at this point given what he knew about his own life. Hopefully his description of the ends would provide Scotty the needed incentive to persevere with the means. "Trust me," he said. "If you don't know much about them now, you'll want to by the time I'm through."

Steamrolling Scotty's skepticism, Scott proceeded to carefully describe the advances computers would make in the not-too-distant future—explaining, as best he knew, just where and when such advances would take place, including the development of the Internet, and how it would explode into an essential part of millions of businesses and homes all around the world. It was obvious from the look on Scotty's face that he was skeptical, but at the same time he didn't interrupt, which Scott took as a good sign.

Scott then focused on his idea for the crux of this third and final alteration of his past: computer viruses. Unlike Internet-based companies, he explained, which would come and go, these overlooked strings of computer code would likely infiltrate computers into the indefinite future—crashing systems and wreaking havoc on universities and colleges around the world, on large and small businesses alike . . .

Scott stopped talking, his mind suddenly wrestling with this last thought. Something about it bothered him, but exactly what it was eluded him.

Scotty nudged his shoulder. "You okay?"

Scott shrugged and resumed talking, assuring Scotty that he believed viruses, or at least the fear of them, would always exist. "Few were prepared for the damage these tiny programs caused, Scotty. If you joined those on the forefront of combating this danger—maybe even creating a company of your own—you'd make millions." He looked his younger self square in the eye. "Millions, Scotty," he repeated.

The two talked for more than an hour, Scott urging him to pursue a scholarship, to use football if he could, to help pave his way to success. He'd need all the help he could get to enter the kind of college Scott had in mind. He encouraged Scotty to talk with a school counselor—something he himself had never done—to help him find a school on the cutting edge of computer technology. He offered a few suggestions of his own, but figured a counselor would provide better options. After all, though he used computers frequently at work, and still enjoyed tinkering with them as a hobby, Scott knew he was by no means an expert on the subject.

They also debated Scotty's dislike of computers; it was clearly an outgrowth of Scotty's change in social status. Scott admitted he had never been a prodigy when it came to such things, but stressed the importance of vision and direction. All Scotty needed to do, he pointed out, was enter the computer programming realm and steer those with the brains in the proper direction—leadership alone could be more powerful than any one specific skill.

It was only after he finally described the financial struggles of his own present that the youth ultimately conceded that the career choice Scott was recommending did seem a far more attractive alternative.

"You'll never have to worry about money again, Scotty."

Scott wondered how much sense these final words really made, given that his younger self was still living at home with his mother and didn't seem to worry about money now. But Scotty nodded, seeming to grasp what he meant by it.

"All right. I'll do my best. It does sound promising." He sounded truly sincere.

Scott stood and offered his hand for the final time. "You have drive and determination. Use them, Scotty."

"Thanks." The young man hesitantly took his hand. Scott reflected on how unaware he was of how much Scotty's life had been changed as a result of listening to his older self. Unaware, as well, that this was the third and final change. *Should I mention that?* he wondered. In the end he decided against it.

As they parted, Scott couldn't help throwing out one more piece of advice. "And, hey, Scotty." The young man looked over his shoulder, his smooth and confident persona already reemerging. "Show a little more respect for the girls, huh?"

Scotty smirked, giving a knowing laugh. He then turned and jogged back toward the school building—no doubt very tardy for his next class.

"Are you satisfied with your third change, Scott?" asked the guardian.

Scott was slightly bothered by the boy's youthful cockiness, but he had to admit that he was very content. "I am. I really am. I've managed to correct three areas in my life I've always been unhappy with: I stand up for myself, it's clear I'm more popular, and, soon, I'll be a lot wealthier than I am now." He folded his arms. "Thanks, Guardian. It's been interesting. Fun."

As Scotty disappeared through the door of the nearest building, Scott chuckled, feeling genuinely pleased with the outcome of his changes. "Not bad," he congratulated himself. "Not bad at all."

After a moment of silence, the guardian acknowledged Scott's self-satisfaction. "You bring to mind a thought I once heard," he observed, somewhat somberly.

Scott reluctantly left off daydreaming about what his life would have been like if such changes really were possible. "What was that?" he asked, still distracted.

"A truly wise man respects the strength of his own hand, wary of its potential when left to his own learning and desire," the guardian quoted.

Something in the words caught Scott's attention, but he hadn't really focused on listening and had missed the meaning. "What are you trying to say, Guardian?"

The voice was solemn. "Be careful what you wish for."

CHAPTER 12

The black nothingness had returned. "Guardian?"

"I'm still here, Scott."

"So, what happens now? I've made my three changes."

"You have."

"So now what?" Scott repeated.

"Well, the rules now change slightly. You may continue moving forward in time to whatever point you wish, but you won't have an influence on your younger self."

Scott realized how much he had been enjoying himself. He didn't know how much longer this incredible experience would last, but he was still intrigued by its possibilities.

Gone, for now, were questions regarding how everything he'd experienced was possible. He had grown to trust the strange voice. More importantly, he had formed an emotional attachment to his younger self, and was developing quite a curiosity regarding the effects his three changes would have on his life. Scott still wasn't quite sure what these changes meant for him personally, but he at least wanted to observe how fulfilling and rewarding they would be for his younger self—the self that he had helped to mold.

"So, can I go forward as often as I want?" he asked. "Or do I have to give you three specific periods, like I did before?"

"The changes have already been made, Scott. There is no need for limitations regarding time, place, or how many visits into your future you can make now. All you have to tell me is where in time you would like to go first."

"Will I be able to talk to those I come in contact with?"

"I wouldn't recommend it," was the guardian's only response.

Scott was silent for quite some time, thinking. He knew the guardian wouldn't interrupt him—his patience seemed limitless.

He paced back and forth on his floor of nothing, and gave careful consideration to where—when—he wanted to go next. It seemed such a simple question: If he could go to any time he wanted, when would he go? The words were simple, but the possibilities were limitless! Would he witness once more the births of his children? Would he visit a loved one prior to their death? Would he want to see his own death, to find out when and how it was to occur?

His first instinct was simply to jump ahead fourteen or so years to see himself at his present age—that would simplify comparing his current life with the supposedly altered one. How did Kate enjoy living on easy street? What did his mom think of all the changes he'd made? He'd nearly settled on that idea. But it was this latter thought that suddenly triggered a memory he had often reflected on with pride. And although he risked this mind-bending experience ending at any moment without satisfying his curiosity, he did long to replay, in the vivid detail he'd experienced thus far, the *one* moment in time when he knew he'd truly made his mother happy and proud. He suddenly made the decision.

"All right, Guardian, I'm ready," Scott called out.

"Where and when would you like to go first?" the guardian asked promptly.

"I'd like to jump forward three years from my last visit." Out loud he thought the request sounded strange.

"Why only three?" the guardian sounded almost surprised.

It brought a full smile to Scott's face. "It was the first time I felt on top of the world in my mother's eyes."

"You'll have to be a bit more specific, Scott."

"I want to revisit the day I arrived home from my mission. You know, of course, that my dad died from cancer when I was young. Mom was always concerned, not having a father around, that I wouldn't have the desire to serve a mission—my father hadn't been able to because of Vietnam. I don't know why it bothered her so much. I had plenty of role models around me in church and Scouting. But then, I was her only child, and I suppose that's normal for a single parent . . . I don't know."

"I see. Any particular location, part of the day?"

Scott grinned once more. "That's easy—at the airport, the moment I stepped off the plane."

Never would he forget the look in his mother's eyes. Not only had she been proud of him and the accomplishment those two years represented, but he could tell she was also proud of herself. As a parent, she had pulled it off—*she* had succeeded in her own mind, as well.

He wanted, suddenly longed, to see that day more than any other event, once more—to take it all in one more time while he could.

"Very well, Scott," the guardian said.

In a flash, Scott found himself standing in a near-empty concourse of the Salt Lake City airport.

Large white letters and numbers labeled the gates on either side of him. The gate at the far end of the concourse was clearly his, for it was the only gate with a profusion of family, friends, and balloons in front of it.

The darkened windows revealed night all around him, an overhead clock reminding him how late his plane had arrived. How many times had he changed planes before arriving in Utah? Four? And he would never forget the six-hour layover in Denver—so close to being home and yet so far away.

Scott started toward the gate at the sight of an airplane slowly taxiing alongside the building. He was sure it was his and was anxious to find a good position from which to watch everything. He chose a corner near the gate, where he had a good view of the door but wouldn't collide with any of the many milling people.

He carefully scanned the crowd looking for his mother. He couldn't find her at first, but it was a large crowd. He'd locate her eventually.

A couple of minutes later a cheer erupted from several people as the first missionary, amidst a weary string of red-eyed passengers, rounded a corner in the disembarking walkway and passed through the terminal door.

Elder Hodges! thought Scott. *Boy, does he look young!* Scott recalled how he had wanted to be the first one from their group off the plane. Pride in having achieved that goal was clearly written all over Hodges's face. Scott thought if Hodges smiled any harder his face might turn inside out. Hodges was soon swallowed up by family members anxious for a hug, forcing Scott to stand on his toes in an attempt to see beyond the crowd.

A bouquet of balloons blocked most of his view for several minutes, but he reminded himself that he'd been one of the last to exit the plane. He was sure he still had a few minutes to wait.

Scott spent those few remaining minutes continuing to search for his mother, so as to catch her expression the moment he *did* arrive. But with so many families huddled together, moving and shuffling about, he soon gave up even that. He'd follow his younger self to her when the time came.

The crowd came to life again as Elders Miller, Hastings, and Jenson emerged, each welcomed with as much fanfare and energy as Hodges had been.

There had been seven in his group, if he remembered right, so he shouldn't have much longer to wait. Again he searched the crowd for the only familiar face that had been there to welcome him home.

Later he had learned that his mother had insisted upon it—she alone would pick him up at the airport, and together they would make the long drive home. A larger celebration awaited him the following day, but his mother had wanted to celebrate his welcome home alone. The long drive gave them plenty of time to chat; his mother had wanted to be the first to hear all about her boy's incredible adventure. In his mother's eyes, they had struggled and longed for this day together, and *together* is how she had wanted to celebrate its completion. Scott smiled fondly at the memory.

Elder Jackson emerged next. He had gained nearly fifty pounds on his mission, and his suit wasn't about to let him forget it. Everyone had tried to talk him into wearing something else, Scott recalled, but he'd insisted on wearing home the same suit he'd left in. His slacks hadn't been about to conform to his nearly impossible desire—a fairly new pair ended up replacing them—but his suit coat was doing its best to comply. Scott smiled. He just hoped Jackson wouldn't end up hugging someone too tightly. There was only thread holding that coat together—not quarter-inch cable.

Scott's attention was distracted from the door by several missionaries introducing their families to one another and snapping last pictures of each other. The nostalgia he felt just watching them nearly choked him. He blinked and went back to watching the door.

Elder Parker appeared next—thin as a rail and as emotional as a soap opera. *I must have been behind him,* thought Scott.

Scott was feeling almost desperate now. He would be coming through the door any second. He irrationally wondered if the scene would replay itself correctly even if he hadn't spotted his mother in time.

The stream of passengers, though, eventually died out, and the crowd of family and friends began to dissipate.

He hadn't seen any sign of his mother, let alone himself.

A feeling of complete emptiness filled his heart as the door to the walkway closed. His mind clouded over with shock as the last of the friends and families eventually left the concourse altogether—undoubtedly headed for the baggage claim . . . and then home.

The terminal fell into near silence as even the ticket agents left the desk; the next flight was apparently not scheduled until some time later.

Only a handful of people remained in the terminal. An older woman in the distance, pushing a large vacuum cleaner, was the only person headed in his direction.

Anger began to boil within him at the guardian's taciturnity.

"Is this some kind of a joke?" he spat out. "What happened? Did you neglect to tell me I missed my plane?"

The guardian responded promptly. He sounded unhappy. "It's no joke, Scott. I promise I wouldn't do that to you for something this important." Scott heard the guardian sigh. "The fact is you didn't serve a mission."

Scott pushed his shock at that revelation aside, reaching instead for his anger. He ran his hands through his hair in frustration. "Then why bring me here?" he demanded.

"You asked me to. And, as with the rocket, you seemed so confident this would still have taken place," began the guardian. "Your mission had been an important milestone in your life, Scott. You needed to fully understand that it no longer exists."

Scott swallowed, feeling numb and unsure. What had seemed entertaining only minutes earlier was now nightmarishly different.

"It was difficult for your mother, but she's never stopped believing in you, Scott."

At the mention of his mother, the suggestion that she had in some way been hurt by all this nonsense, Scott bristled. "All right, look! Enough of this!" he shouted. What few people remained in the terminal suddenly looked in his direction. He ignored all of them. "I want out, all right? You've had your fun, now let's end it!"

Even louder he shouted, "Do you hear me, Scott?" He called out to himself, "Wake up!" For the entire experience, Scott had maintained his tacit belief that he was only experiencing one of the most vivid dreams he'd ever had in his life. It was still the only explanation that really made any sense to him.

"Sir? Can I get something for you?"

Startled, Scott turned, his eyes locking with those of the janitor. She wore a genuine look of concern.

Scott threw up his hands. "This is ridiculous!" he shouted into the air. *None of this can be real,* he told himself. He glared into the woman's eyes. "*You* aren't even real!" he yelled.

Her expression switched immediately to fear, and she took an involuntary step backward.

Frustrated, Scott backed away himself and then began walking briskly toward the escalator of the main terminal. *This is absurd. It's stupid!* he thought.

"Do you really still believe this is a dream, Scott?" he heard the guardian's voice ask.

"Shut up!" Scott snapped.

A large, heavyset man, huffing and wheezing as he walked by Scott, glared at him, adjusting the strap of his large carry-on bag. Scott ignored him.

"Haven't you noticed the changes that have already taken place?" the guardian tried. "Surely you must see that you're not the same young man you once were."

Scott tried to ignore the voice, tried to force it out of his mind, but it surrounded him—penetrated his very being.

I'm losing it, Scott concluded. *I'm honestly losing it! Why did I go along with any of this? It's a nightmare—a glorified nightmare!*

"Where shall we go now, Scott?" the guardian sounded as patient and as friendly as ever, but Scott refused to respond. With everything crumbling around him, Scott couldn't help feeling anger toward the guardian. Patience sounded patronizing at the moment.

I have to snap out of this, he thought frantically to himself. *There has to be some way for me to wake up!*

He caught sight of a public restroom to his right and headed for it. "Scott?" called the guardian.

It was probably absurd to use something from what he concluded had to be his own imagination to try to snap himself out of this, but he honestly didn't know what else to try. Willing himself awake obviously hadn't worked.

"Scott? Slow down. Let's talk about this, shall we?"

The restroom appeared empty, and he rushed for one of the many sinks lining the east wall. He turned on the cold water and began splashing it on his face.

"As hard as this might be for you, we must continue, Scott," the guardian informed him.

Scott's head shot up, the faucet continuing to run while he stared at his wet reflection in the large mirror on the wall. "Look, this is a dream. So back off!" he said loudly.

"I thought we'd settled that, Scott. I've told you many times that this is not simply a dream."

Scott clenched his fists. "Enough!" he yelled, pounding the sink with his right fist for emphasis.

"Scott, listen to me. Dreams are often nothing more than random bits of memory and thought, haphazardly thrown together by your own subconscious mind and imagination."

Scott continued splashing cold water onto his face, trying to summon a giant pool of water he could dive into instead.

"Ask yourself, Scott. Has any of this seemed randomly generated to you? Have you ever had this much control over your own thoughts and actions within a dream before?"

Scott only shook his head. *A dream!* he insisted to himself. *There's no other explanation for it! It* has *to be a . . .* Scott abruptly clenched his wet jaw—his mind latching onto the only life preserver he had left.

He slowly shut off the water. "There's only one sensation a dream can't reproduce, isn't there?" he managed from between clenched teeth. He was staring hard into his own reflection. It hadn't been a question as much as it was Scott's desperate desire to hold on to his sanity.

"What is that, Scott?" the voice sounded weary.

"Pain. You can't experience physical pain in a dream. At least I never have." He flexed his right hand and then balled it into an even tighter fist.

"If you say so, Scott."

"*That's* what I thought!" And with everything he had, his pulled back and punched his own reflection.

The mirror shattered around Scott's fist, as did two of Scott's knuckles. The pain of the blow jolted Scott to the core.

He gasped, his breathing suddenly labored as he pulled his broken hand into his chest. The pain sent a wave of nausea through him that rapidly brought him to his knees.

He looked down at his right hand, cradling it with his left. The skin over the knuckles had split to the bone, and blood trickled onto his jeans as well as onto the restroom's gray, tile floor.

What's . . . what's happening to me? he thought. *How can this be?*

Scott's mind was reeling; the pain seemed unbearable. But even more troubling and deeply disturbing was the undeniable, terrifying realization that the voice had once and for all been right: This *wasn't* a dream.

CHAPTER 13

"But I don't feel like singing."
"I know it's hard, dear. But don't you think he'd appreciate it?"
"I don't know."
"Well, I know he would. Now, come on, honey. What's your favorite carol?"
"But—"
"Come on. You must have a favorite."
"Away in a Manger?'"
"Great choice! Okay. Are you ready?"
"I guess."
"All right. Together. 'Away in a manger, no crib for his bed' . . ."

* * *

Scott became aware that he was lying on his back. His eyes were open. The reason he couldn't see anything was that he had returned to the black nothingness.

He realized his hand didn't hurt anymore, so he sat up to look in wonderment at the skin surrounding his once torn and bloody knuckles. His hand looked just as it had before. There was no sign of injury—not even a scratch or scar left behind. He rotated his wrist several times before carefully flexing his fingers. All the pain had disappeared.

What in the world has happened to me? he thought, as he turned around. He could still see only the black of nothingness, but he now looked at it with new eyes. *Where am I?*

Scott slowly got to his feet, a renewed sense of fear and curiosity struggling against newfound awe and wonder. It was beyond words. He simply had no explanation for what had happened—was happening—to him.

"Are you all right, Scott?" asked the guardian. The voice was comforting, yet now it seemed more mysterious than ever.

Scott's gaze returned to his hand and he flexed it once more. "I . . ." He just didn't know what to say, or even what to feel. "I broke it . . . my hand . . . didn't I?"

"You did, Scott. Now it's been healed," the guardian said simply.

For no reason that he could legitimize, Scott didn't question the answer. He simply nodded. The whys and hows of the moment evaporated under a clear, if twisted, sense of logic. *It's been healed*, he repeated to himself. That did *sound* right.

Scott sat back down and began replaying the incident over in his mind. This time he was not questioning the reality of any of it. Instead, his mind seemed capable of pondering only a few aspects of it.

"The janitor," he began quietly.

"You had no desire to hurt that woman, and you left as soon as you realized you were scaring her. She will retain no lasting effects from the incident."

The irony of the situation hadn't escaped Scott. "My actions could easily have been dismissed as those of a crazy man," he concluded.

"I suppose that's true," the guardian agreed. "But you don't believe you're crazy, do you, Scott?"

Scott seriously considered that for a moment. It would definitely explain everything he was now going through—wouldn't it? The flashbacks, the strange voice in his head, the sudden shifting of reality. But it seemed too convenient an excuse. The voice had been right earlier—if this was indeed simply his mind turning inside out on him, how could he possibly have so much control over his thoughts and actions now? If he was genuinely going insane, would he have the ability to even ask that question?

Surprisingly confident in the logic of his thoughts, Scott gave the only answer he felt made any sense, "No. I don't think I'm crazy."

He stood once more and slowly slid his hands into his pockets, surveying the emptiness around him. He didn't *feel* crazy. He felt shaken up, confused, and disoriented, maybe, but not crazy. He still had control of his thoughts and reasoning abilities—he was sure of it. In that case, only one other conclusion was possible.

His voice was somber as he phrased his next question. "What I just saw . . . it happened?"

"It did," the guardian confirmed.

A small part of Scott still wanted to lash out at the voice, calling it on such an obvious lie. But how could he possibly deny what he'd just experienced? The pain *had* been real. The people and images had been too clear and consistent to be anything but reality. He recalled that often, whenever he had had a dream where writing was visible, whether it be a book he was trying to read or signs he was trying to make sense of, the letters and words always seemed to shift in his dream. They never stayed still and he'd always been irritated with his inability to focus and read within a dream. Yet, he *had* been able to do that at the airport. In fact, he could remember some of the exact cities he'd noticed on the airport's scheduling monitors, and the numbers on the gates within the concourse. They hadn't shifted in his mind, as those in a dream might; they behaved as true memories that he could recall as easily as anything else.

Scott shook his head. *Maybe he's right,* he conceded. *Maybe this IS real.* As quickly as this admission came to his mind, Scott felt flooded with acceptance of everything the guardian had been telling him. It all, for some reason, just felt . . . correct. To his surprise, he found himself beginning to accept such a possibility, though, at the same time, he felt a sudden discomfort in his stomach. *If I had . . . changed things, what do I do now?*

"Where and when shall we go now, Scott?" asked the guardian.

For a moment Scott couldn't help feeling a bit irritated. The guardian was apparently ready to simply move on, but Scott was still trying to grasp all that his sudden shift in perception entailed. "Just . . . hold it, will you?" he snapped.

Scott brought his hands to the sides of his head and massaged his temples, shutting his eyes against the inevitability of yet another . . . *Another what?* he wondered. *I still haven't the foggiest idea what to call these events.*

Since he couldn't make sense out of his current situation, he began trying to make sense out of what he'd just witnessed at the airport. It was at least a start.

"So," he finally said, "you're telling me I . . . I didn't serve a mission."

"That is correct."

Scott closed his eyes once more and took a slow, deep breath before asking his follow-up question. "If I . . ." How could he phrase it? "If . . . If I didn't serve a mission . . . then what did I . . . what did I do?"

"Scotty followed your advice, of course," responded the guardian matter-of-factly.

"My advice?"

"Of course, Scott." The guardian paused. "Well, for the most part."

Scott's eyes opened. "What do you mean 'for the most part?'"

"He did just what you told him to do. The very next day he made an appointment with the school counselor, who steered him toward the University of Southern California. There he played for the Trojans with a quarter scholarship while—under academic probation—taking classes and managing to rub shoulders with some of the key pioneers in computer-virus research—Fred Cohen, himself, as a matter of fact."

Scott was stunned. "You're telling me that I became a programmer that quickly?"

"Not exactly. You started out in that direction, but discovered you just didn't have what it took to compete with . . . 'the geeks,' as you called them."

"So what did I do?" Scott was confused.

"Scotty dropped the idea of pursuing programming, and opted for a few business classes instead, remembering well your advice regarding leadership being more powerful than any one specific skill. Remember, Scott?"

Of course he remembered. He remembered it very well. And the very fact that he could remember it all, word for word, seemed to further validate everything the guardian told him.

"So, I . . . dropped out?" Scott asked.

"Are you surprised?"

"It's just that I—"

"Scott, ask yourself this: What was the first thing you truly felt you'd actually *finished* in your life? The one event that convinced you that you could accomplish anything if you honestly set your mind to it?"

He knew the answer, but refused to voice it.

"It was your mission, Scott. Wasn't it? Up to that point in your life, completing a mission was the largest goal you'd ever seen clear to the end."

Scott stubbornly remained silent, but the voice continued anyway.

"Scotty held on to several 'geeks,' encouraging them in their studies and rewarding them with the benefits his popularity and charm attracted—all the while promising to include them in a programming idea that would make them immensely wealthy. They bought into it. It was that simple.

"Scotty managed a brief apprenticeship with a reputable business firm, and carefully began acquiring the information to start an independent business. Soon he dropped out of the internship and the university altogether.

"After he and his programming *friends* opened their own business, they had to convince a jittery public that their antivirus software, the first of its kind, was precisely what the proverbial doctor ordered."

Silence stretched after the guardian stopped speaking.

Scott was stunned. How could his younger self have put so much together so fast?

Then, as if reading his mind, the voice concluded, "Greed, like desire, is a persuasive motivator, Scott—pushing men to accomplish incredible feats. Unfortunately, what's 'right' often gets pushed aside in favor of what's lucrative."

Scott brushed that comment aside. He was still trying to comprehend that he hadn't served a mission. Finally the question came. "If I wasn't at the airport . . . where was I that night?"

"I'm glad you asked."

A darkened office suddenly leaped into view.

CHAPTER 14

Scott had been completely unprepared for the change, and was breathing heavily, unsure if he could really handle another round of this. But all was quiet, and the darkened windows assured him it was late at night, the large and vacant office obviously closed for the evening. He stood there, taking the time he needed to orient himself to his new surroundings. He peered around in the darkness at the faint outline of filing cabinets and chest-high cubicle walls.

He became aware of a faint tapping—or the clicking sound of a computer keyboard—to his left. He found himself standing against a wall with a couple of large filing cabinets at his immediate right, while a hallway opened up just a few feet to his left.

Cautiously, he peered around the corner and down the hallway. "Can anybody see or hear me here, Guardian?" he whispered.

"Not at the moment," replied the guardian at his normal volume, startling Scott. Scott grimaced to himself and moved toward the typing sound.

The hallway ran only a short distance before opening up into three offices: one on the left, one on the right—both of their doors closed—and one directly in front of him. Its door stood halfway open. Soft light from a desk lamp spilled from the opening onto the hallway floor.

Beyond the doorway Scott could see a young man, his back to him, typing industriously away at a keyboard. The typing stopped and Scott saw the back of the young man's head grow still. *He must be reading over what he's just typed.* Though he couldn't make an absolutely positive identification from where he was standing, Scott had little doubt as to the young man's identity. *It's me,* he thought. *I'm sure of it.*

After a few minutes the young man in the chair—Scott still thought of him as Scotty—leaned back and clasped his hands behind his head. "That ought to do it," he muttered. He tapped at the keyboard a few more times.

A loud, obnoxious dot-matrix printer slashed at the silence, abruptly stopping after printing what had to have been only a few lines of text.

His younger self let out a string of curses and stood up. "I'm always having to put a fresh ribbon in this thing!"

Scott flattened himself to the wall outside the office as Scotty passed by him, heading, no doubt, for a supply closet to get a new printer ribbon.

Scott watched the young man walk to the outer edge of the cubicles and then down an aisle and through a door on the far side of the large office space. Then he stepped through the doorway and located Scotty's computer monitor. The blinking white cursor stood out vividly against the document's blue background. It was blinking right next to the title of the document.

"It's the business plan he'll show the loan officer he's meeting with tomorrow," explained the guardian.

The voice nearly sent Scott to the ceiling, and it took a few seconds for him to collect himself before he could return to skimming the document. He knew no one else could hear the voice, but the way in which it penetrated his very being in the quiet stillness always shocked him. He resolved to be less jumpy.

Scott quickly skimmed what he could see of the document. He thought about arrowing down through the rest of it, but didn't want to risk the noise the older keyboard might make.

From what he did read, however, it was obvious that Scotty had done his homework. It would begin as a small start-up company, but was estimated to grow rapidly as the threat of and panic over computer viruses spread worldwide.

"It's estimated, Scott, that he'll make two million his first year, and at least thirty million over the next three," the guardian added.

His curiosity was simply too much for him. Scott pressed the "page down" button once. Sure enough, a distinct click followed. He pressed the key once more.

Scott's eyes found the figures he'd been looking for. After a few seconds, he straightened, overwhelmed at the company's projected success—greater than even *he* had imagined.

He noticed on the wall a USC pennant, as well as several framed newspaper clippings highlighting Trojan team wins. But he didn't focus on them.

Thirty million! He shook his head at the thought of such a fortune and, for a brief instant, brightened. *A man could do a lot of good in this world with thirty million dollars!* But on the heels of this thought suddenly came a memory of the Gutierrez family back in Guatemala. The father had tears in his eyes as he expressed his thanks to Scott for bringing the gospel to them.

The Gutierrezes's hand-built shelter had been just that—shelter. A single light bulb hanging from the ceiling was their only source of light at night. And, with the help of a small adapter, the fixture was their electricity source during the day. A few pieces of vinyl-wrapped, iron-bar furniture, and cinder blocks—painted, of course—were all they had with which to fill the tiny living space. The blocks served as tables, chairs—whatever was needed at the time. A couple of mattresses in the next room completed the furnishings. He remembered well the hose and stone sink in back that served as both kitchen sink and washing machine. The Gutierrez family, like others in Guatemala, struggled to simply survive.

But they never complained. Their children played with scraps of leather given them by their father, a shoemaker by trade. The sewing machine he used was old but well cared for—clearly the vital centerpiece of their humble home.

The tears in the man's eyes had been genuine, and Scott's throat tightened with the memory. *A poor but loving family,* he would have described them.

"I'm now a rich man!" Brother Gutierrez had said after being confirmed. And Scott remembered thinking, at the time, how right the man was. He cared for and protected his family, as every father should. Now, if they lived righteously, their family would be eternal.

He'd met hundreds of men just like Brother Gutierrez while on his mission. He had truly been a witness to the most desperate poverty. But that was precisely the problem. *He* had experienced it—

Scotty hadn't . . . and wouldn't. Scotty would not feel the need to help a family like that with his money.

It occurred to Scott to wonder how the memories of *his* life hadn't changed. He remembered his childhood and mission, his career, family, and kids—everything. He could think back on them as well as anybody else at this stage of life, he supposed. And he had made changes that only seemed to be affecting Scotty's life; Scott's memories remained untouched.

How long would that last?

Surely these changes he was making would eventually begin affecting his own memories, wouldn't they? Like some distant tsunami brewing offshore, would all of his changes eventually come crashing down at some point, washing away any previous memories he had?

Was that possible? Scott didn't know what was possible anymore.

His throat tightened even more. *I swore I'd never forget what I learned on my mission,* he thought helplessly. His eyes began to fill with tears as he remembered how he'd promised himself that when he was a father he'd remember his mission and always be grateful for whatever he had—always value what was *really* important. The people of Guatemala had provided the perfect object lesson—what he had thought was an unforgettable lesson.

Only now, he had forgotten it, and Scotty would never learn it; he would never be aware of all of the lives he had . . . *could* have touched, as well as all of the lives that could have touched his.

For a moment Scott found himself wondering if the Gutierrez family, like his mother, had also been affected by these changes, but quickly dismissed it; it was simply too overwhelming to contemplate. He consoled himself that surely another missionary had found them. He didn't want to think about whether that was true.

Scott again glanced at the figures on the screen. He felt sick inside. *Can any amount of money ever replace the rewards of a faithful mission?*

He closed his eyes as he heard the sound of a distant door closing. Scotty was returning to his office.

Scott let out his breath in a long sigh. *What have I done?*

He heard the footfalls heading in his direction. Scott didn't feel like seeing Scotty again. In a quiet voice, Scott simply said, "Please, Guardian, just take me home."

CHAPTER 15

"Well?"

"No change."

"But I thought you said—"

"I know. I'm sorry. I was wrong."

"But then, how long will it be?"

"At this point, there's no way of guessing. A week, a month. We'll just have to wait and see. I know how hard this must be for you, but—"

"No! No, you don't know. You . . . you have no idea!"

* * *

The deep tone of a grandfather clock's half-hour chime startled Scott. He opened his eyes.

He found himself standing in the vestibule of what had to be a mansion of considerable size. From the large and delicately crafted chandelier high overhead to the genuine white marble floor beneath his feet, everything around him bespoke fine taste and fortune.

"Where am I?" he asked, taking a few cautious steps and craning his neck in an attempt to see what might be atop the plush, carpeted, circular staircase that began spiraling off to his right.

"Your house," answered the guardian.

"My what?"

"Your house, Scott. This is where you currently live."

Scott's heartbeat quickly overtook the steady ticking of the tall crystal clock to his left. "You mean, at age thirty-four . . . this is where I live?"

"That's correct."

"But I told you to take me . . ." There was little point in arguing. He had asked to be taken home and, of course, he *had* been—to Scotty's home.

Scott resigned himself to his surroundings and quietly made his way toward what appeared to be the living room.

"Don't worry. No one can hear you, There's no one here. Feel free to look around, Scott."

Scott was surprised to find himself greatly relieved by these words. He just didn't feel like meeting up with anyone. After only a handful of steps, he found himself standing within the largest living room he had ever seen.

Absorbed in the majesty around him, Scott was able to put aside, for the moment, all of the dark and disturbing thoughts he'd felt only minutes earlier. The sunlight alone, streaming through large, wall-length windows, did wonders to enliven and awaken his weary spirit.

Several long couches, some white leather, some fabric, lined the center and outer regions of the room. Scattered throughout were short bookcases and end tables supporting a wide variety of statuary and antique artifacts. All of the couches faced an impressive stone fireplace that nearly filled an entire wall.

Set into the stone a few feet above the hearth was a large wide-screen television, with speakers and stereo equipment taking up the remainder of the wall space beyond the edges of the stone. The opening of a hallway directly to his left promised even more space beyond the stone.

High above his head was the vaulted ceiling and track lighting illuminating hanging works of modern art—giving one the sense of being in a museum rather than a home.

The wall opposite the vestibule seemed to be made almost entirely of glass, and the majestic view of pine-covered mountains created an illusion of living in the trees rather than on the ground.

An enormous kitchen and dining room opened up to his right. Masterfully crafted woodwork disguised all the major appliances, while the chrome fixtures appeared highlighted amidst countertops of polished granite.

Above the living room ran an exposed hallway, ending in what Scott assumed to be a bedroom, bounded by glass, above the kitchen.

Scott counted two doors off the hallway before it disappeared beyond the stone wall of the fireplace.

"I *live* here?" he repeated in disbelief.

"You do."

"It's . . . it's incredible."

"Look around some more, Scott," invited the guardian. "No one's going to care if you do."

Scott nodded and slowly made his way farther into the living room. He spent the next twenty minutes exploring the many rooms of the ground floor. He found a laundry room, storage room, office, and sitting room. The massive game room and gym he hadn't been expecting at all. It was clear by the condition of some of the weights that they'd followed him from his high school football days. In another spacious room, he found a good-sized indoor swimming pool, hot tub, and steam room—the humid air wafting the faint scent of chlorine past his nose.

Finding the door to the garage, he couldn't help smiling over the fact that his taste in cars hadn't changed, and he admired for several minutes the fully restored '65 Stingray, appearing showroom-fresh under the bright light of the spacious four-car garage—tuxedo black with leather interior and tinted windows. It was gorgeous.

He shut the driver's-side door after exploring its interior. "Did I restore it?" He hadn't seen any real evidence in the garage of the tools and equipment needed to accomplish such a task, but maybe he had a second workroom.

"No, Scott. This is the condition it was in when you bought it."

Scott felt oddly let down. This fact diminished the value of the car for him. The owner of a car such as this ought to be able to handle its upkeep and maintenance. *But, then, if you're rich enough,* thought Scott, *who cares?*

Scott considered going outside to take a look at the grounds. But he didn't really see the point. He could already anticipate the manicured lawn, the well-trimmed trees and shrubs, and the expansive yard Scotty undoubtedly enjoyed. Instead, Scott shut off the lights in the garage and made his way back to the living room.

"Well? What do you think?" asked the guardian.

"It's amazing," he said without much enthusiasm. What else could he say?

"Yes, and kept very tidy, wouldn't you say?"

"Sure, but I'll bet we've got a team of maids, landscapers, and mechanics on hand to take care of it all. We'd have to with a place this size."

"You do have help with the maintenance of the grounds, of course. But you have only one maid. She comes in twice a week."

"Oh, please," began Scott. "A place like this . . ." He stopped just short of the living room, in full view of the furnishings and decor.

Several seconds passed.

"What is it, Scott?" the guardian finally asked.

Something wasn't right. Slowly Scott walked to the nearest couch, running his fingers absentmindedly over the elegant, unblemished arm.

His eyes darted from the bright white walls to the undisturbed magazines on one of the two coffee tables beside him. With a maid, he could understand why the walls might be free of dirty fingerprints. But the undisturbed magazines . . . *that* was the tip-off!

Scott jogged quickly to the spiral staircase within the vestibule, taking the steps two at a time until he'd reached the second floor. His final step placed him in front of what he had correctly assumed to be a bedroom. He ignored the king-sized bed, plush carpeting, and displayed artwork, and headed straight for the closets.

Throwing open all of the many-mirrored bi-fold doors, he stood staring at the vast array of suits, ties, sports jackets, and shoes that filled the closets.

He then rushed to the large oak dressers and yanked open each drawer, now frantic in his search.

Still holding onto the handle of the last open drawer, he froze. He stared down at its contents, breathing heavily, unable to focus on anything in the drawer.

After several minutes, he dragged himself to the foot of the enormous bed, sat down, and buried his head in his hands.

Tears began to flow.

He raised his red-rimmed eyes to study the near-bare, sterile walls. The pictures that did hang there were abstract images of nothing—lighted symbols without feeling or heart.

Scott finally drew up the courage to ask a question he wasn't sure he wanted to know the answer to. "Where are they?"

"Who, Scott?"

He closed his eyes, forcing himself to remain calm. He took a long, deep breath. "Kate. My wife. My . . ." his voice broke. "My children."

"You never met Kate, Scott."

The implications of the guardian's answer bewildered him, and he felt as if a great weight crushed his heart. His chin slowly dropped to his chest.

"Instead of attending the community college," the guardian explained, "you went to USC, remember? You never had the chance to meet because you weren't there."

Scott tried to digest that. He tried to put all of the illogical, awkwardly fitting pieces of the puzzle together, but couldn't. He had no tangible frame of "reality" to put the pieces into, did he? He honestly didn't know what to believe anymore.

After a long and painful silence, Scott asked, "Where is she?"

"Where's who?"

"Enough, all right?" Scott was furious, his patience completely expended. "Who do you think I mean? My wife!" he shouted. "Kate! Where is Kate? I . . . I want to see her."

"I'm sorry, Scott. I'm really not trying to be difficult. This must be hard on—"

"I want to see her, Guardian," Scott ground out, between clenched teeth.

"But that's impos—"

"Don't tell me what's possible or impossible!" he shouted as he stood, furious at the guardian's hesitation. "Show me my wife, now!"

"Scott, I realize this may be difficult for you to accept, but—"

"Look." Scott rubbed away the tears that had collected on his face. "It's obvious I'm being slapped in the face with the consequences of my decisions. I can *see* that. But we were—*are*—husband and wife, for crying out loud!" He paused a moment as he attempted to calm himself. Only after several deep breaths did Scott try once more. "She's my wife, Guardian. I . . . have the right to know where she is. Show me the consequence, please."

Silence.

"Well?" Scott prompted impatiently.

"I've told you before that you aren't permitted to make any changes at this point in—"

Scott's hands cut through the air as if physically throwing aside the guardian's words. "I have no *doubt* you'll pull me before I cross *any* line," he growled.

Silence.

"I have the right," he muttered again. "I have . . . the right."

After some time the guardian spoke again. "All right, Scott. I suppose you do."

CHAPTER 16

The house that materialized wasn't large by any means. It looked to be a small, comfortable home with a yard to match. A narrow line of flowers traced the short path leading from the driveway to the front door, and Scott's heart tightened at this sign of Kate's handiwork. *Petunias and snapdragons,* he thought. *She always plants petunias and snapdragons.*

Scott didn't recognize the suburb. For all he knew, he could be in a completely different state. It seemed like a nice neighborhood though.

"What is it, Scott?" questioned the guardian.

"I . . ." Scott trailed off without answering.

"You were perhaps expecting more?"

That *had* been his first thought, but he remained silent, his eyes drawn to two boys playing basketball several houses down, while a smaller child—a girl, he believed—on a bicycle watched from the sidewalk. It lifted his spirits to see them making the most of the clear, sunny day. He could hear a few lawn mowers running and wondered if it was Saturday.

"How many times did Kate tell you that she was satisfied with what both of you had?"

He didn't want to acknowledge the voice any more than he had to, but Scott couldn't help responding to this comment. "She was being polite."

"Really?" began the guardian. "Well, take a good look around. It looks like this neighborhood's very similar to the one you live in now. It appears to me that, even given a second chance, she was telling you the truth."

And that was it, wasn't it? A second chance. That was precisely what Scott was seeing now. He was no longer a part of Kate's life. She'd had a second chance, whether she was aware of it or not. Why wouldn't she have married someone else?

Someone else. His stomach churned at the thought as he swallowed and again shoved his hands into the pockets of his jeans. Deep down, he knew he wanted to knock on the door. He was afraid to. In fact he wished all of this nonsense would go away—that he could just have his old life back. But he knew that wasn't likely to happen. What he needed to do now was knock on that door. He *had* to. He needed to confront what he'd demanded the voice show him.

Slowly, he made his way up the short path . . . to the two cement steps . . . to the front door.

"Be careful, Scott," warned the guardian.

Scott ignored the voice, taking out his hand only long enough to ring the doorbell.

Several seconds passed, his heart hammering against his chest. Just when he had decided to knock, the door opened . . . and there she was.

"Hi. Can I help you?" she asked.

Scott's mouth opened slightly at the shock of seeing his wife so clearly, so distinctly. The sound of her voice, the beauty of her face, the smile that came so easily for her, made him want to take her in his arms, beg her to help him escape whatever it was he was experiencing. For a second, he thought of doing just that. Yet he knew that he was not alone; the guardian was nearby. And if he wanted this moment to last, he'd have to be careful.

He cleared his throat and was about to speak when a deep voice from behind her called out, "Who's at the door, hon?" When the stranger came up beside her and put his arm around her waist, Scott's heart turned to ice.

"I . . . I," he stammered. *Why does his hand have to be around her waist?* he thought in agony, forcing his throat, mouth, and tongue to form and voice words he knew needed to be said if he was going to be allowed to stay. If his shock lasted any longer . . .

"I . . . was wondering if you could . . . tell me where I could find . . . the elementary school."

The man beside Kate appeared pleasant enough, though he cut her answer short by stepping past her onto the porch. "Sure," he said. Scott noticed Kate's eyes drop slightly before she retreated back into the house. He knew that look. He'd learned early on in his marriage to avoid hurting his wife's feelings that way. Apparently this guy hadn't figured it out yet, or was ignoring her feelings altogether. Her husband pointed down the street. "Go one more block and then turn right. Straight two more blocks and you're there."

"Thanks." She was gone. Scott tried to avoid looking after her, so as not to antagonize this man.

"No problem. You looking to buy the Landing home?"

"What?" Scott felt so rattled he simply wanted to disappear. He just couldn't fathom his wife being with anyone else but him. But he recognized his hurt beginning to turn into anger, and knew he needed to leave before he did something stupid. The sound of the children playing outside reminded him that he did have an audience. And of course there was always the guardian watching from somewhere. Scott doubted he'd get very far even if he did decide to lose his temper.

"Yeah," the imposter responded. "Checking out the schools— most people do that before moving into an area."

Scott cleared his throat. "Uh, yeah. Just looking." All he wanted to do now was run.

"Well, let me put your mind at ease. The teachers are great, the principal's great. I can't really speak for the junior high and high school yet."

When Scott didn't respond immediately to his comment, Kate's husband threw him a curious glance and proceeded to end what was becoming more and more a one-sided conversation. "Well . . . good. It's a nice area. Hope to see you around. Good luck."

And with that, the door shut.

In a daze, Scott made his way down the steps and back to the small path leading to the driveway. When he reached the sidewalk, he couldn't help turning to survey the house once more. "She seems the same, yet different," he muttered.

"How so?" asked the guardian.

Scott bit at his lower lip. He didn't really feel like talking to anyone right now, but the voice was all he had. "I don't know. Something . . . something's missing. Maybe something in her eyes."

"It could be you, Scott."

"What?"

"Oh, don't get me wrong. Her husband's an excellent provider and treats her fairly well, though he's a bit overbearing at times. But though you may not want to believe or admit it, she needed you as much as you needed her. She's happy . . . just not perhaps as happy as she could have been."

Just then the small child—indeed a girl—he'd seen earlier on the bike wobbled to a stop at his side, gently colliding with his leg. He grabbed the handlebars to steady the bike, giving the young girl the chance to get both feet under her. She couldn't have been more than five or six years old. When she brushed her long, brown hair out of her eyes to look up at him, Scott's face went white with shock.

"Soooorry. This is only my second day on a two wheeler," the little girl explained. "I'm doing good, though, don't you think?"

The question was lost on Scott, for it was her face that had his full attention.

Uncomfortable, the young girl took a few steps backward, slipping her handlebars free from Scott's now-weak grasp. She stepped off the bike and, ignoring his stare, walked it to the side of the small pathway he'd just used. She tried putting down the kickstand, but quickly gave up. She laid it down on its side instead, then bounded up the steps, opened the door, and went inside, leaving Scott behind.

"Her face," Scott whispered.

"Cute as a button, isn't she, Scott?" the voice responded cheerfully.

"I see Kate, but . . ."

"But you're missing," the guardian finished.

Suddenly the significance of it struck Scott with full force.

He swallowed hard. Now, more than ever, he wanted to run from what he was being forced to confront.

The guardian put into words his latest realization—the voice haunting, as everything began fading once more.

"Your children, Scott, will never be."

CHAPTER 17

"Come back to me. Please come back . . ."

* * *

Scott was lying down, his eyes closed. The softness beneath him, and the warmth from above, felt so much like a bed—his own bed. It even felt as though his head were resting on a pillow. He kept his eyes closed, basking in the sensation, fearful that the slightest movement would somehow make it all disappear.

But the longer he lay, the more his resolve began to fade.

Cautiously, he moved one of his legs.

It IS a bed! he realized. *And I'm barefoot.*

Scott moved his other leg across the soft sheets and shifted his arm beneath his head, under what he was now sure was a pillow.

He took a deep breath before cautiously opening his eyes. His reading lamp shown above his head, and below it, his alarm clock, its glowing red numbers telling him it was 5:28 A.M. His eyes went from the clock to the bedroom window, where weak light outlined the blinds.

It's my bedroom, came the thought with a start. *It's morning . . . and I'm in my bedroom.*

He chuckled softly to himself, pulling the sheet and blanket tighter around his body. *The whole blasted thing was a dream. It* was *a dream!* He chuckled once more as relief and joy flooded through him all at once. His chuckling soon turned to laughter.

Someone stirred next to him, mumbling something unintelligible. He rolled over slowly so as not to disturb the only person it could possibly be.

His eyes found her. *Kate!* Scott wanted to reach over to hold her. He wanted to pull her close, tell her all about the horrible nightmare he'd just had. But he restrained himself. It was just a nightmare, after all. He wasn't a child. For all he knew, one of the kids had probably gotten her up several times already during the night. At six, the alarm would go off. Why cut her sleep short? He could wait thirty minutes or so.

He lay back, staring at his bedroom ceiling, and shook his head. "It felt so real!" he whispered. "*So* real!"

In fact, the memory of everything he'd experienced lay fresh in his mind even now—every detail . . . every emotion . . . how he had felt seeing Kate with . . . Scott laughed inwardly and turned to look at her once more.

It was just a dream, Scott, he mentally assured himself. *Relax.*

He studied her sleeping face in the filtered early-morning light. Her hair was in disarray and she was completely without makeup; she looked beautiful—absolutely beautiful.

He turned to check the clock, surprised to find that ten minutes had already passed by. *Ten minutes*—he could wait twenty minutes more, he reasoned.

Scott rolled back onto his side, his eyes coming to rest on the bedroom window. He was comfortable; he was home and she'd be awake soon.

Next to him, as if she had read his mind, Kate began to giggle.

Scott didn't roll over. "What's so funny?" he asked over his shoulder, smiling. Maybe he'd accidentally kicked her during the night, laughed, or said something silly in his sleep. If he had, she would be sure to tease him about it over the next day or two.

"Do you remember the pumpkin pie from last Thanksgiving?" she asked, her voice a bit rough with the early hour.

His smile widened. It was so good to hear her voice again. "Yeah, I guess so. What about it?"

She giggled again, her form shaking beside him. He rolled back onto his back, gave her a quick glance, and then asked again, "What about it, sweetheart?"

"Why can't I ever get it into second?" The giggling continued.

"Second?" Scott replied. "What are you talking about?"

Scott felt her body shift, and from the corner of his eye saw that she'd propped her head up under one elbow. "I just don't know which color to use," she said, hilarity still thick in her voice.

He *had* talked in his sleep, and now she must be making fun of him. He rolled over to face the window. "All right, cut me some slack. I had a rough ni—"

"Where's the van?" she interrupted.

"Excuse me?" This time there was no reply. Scott's eyes found the alarm clock—10:30? *What?* . . . The window . . . beige metal blinds now struggled to keep the glaring sunlight at bay.

But when did the sun—

"Why don't you just go away?" shouted Kate, her voice now sounding completely awake. Scott quickly rolled toward her.

"I think your mom would prefer lemon meringue to pumpkin. That's all I'm saying," she continued calmly.

He stared at her. He was about to ask what in the world she was talking about, but stopped short. She was on one elbow, all right, but as she spoke, she wasn't looking into his eyes. She wasn't looking at him at all!

"School shoes," she added. "That's what we need right now. If you'd just work harder we could pay off the bills."

Scott waved his hand in front of her eyes. She didn't blink—seemed oblivious to him even being there. "We'll go Christmas shopping tomorrow," she said matter-of-factly and lay back, placing her hands behind her head on the pillow.

Scott felt his heart rate increasing and could barely hear above the pounding of his pulse in his ears. Tentatively, he reached out to touch Kate's shoulder, sure she was playing some kind of cruel joke. He had thought her above something like this, but—

His hand made contact with her skin, but it was immediately pushed back with a flash and jolt of electricity.

Scott flexed his fingers. "Kate?" His voice was quiet, hopeful. Then, "Kate!" he shouted. Her eyes wouldn't meet his. She began to laugh.

Had they been having a real conversation, or had a joke been told, the laughter would have been music to his ears. It always had been before. But now her laughter, combined with her unfocused eyes, produced a disturbing—chilling—effect instead.

Scott slipped out from beneath the covers. Kate continued to laugh, staring at the ceiling.

What's going on here? he wondered.

His eyes shot back to the blinds. It was dark behind them.

"Daddy?"

The distant sound of his seven-year-old daughter from the end of the hallway, beyond his bedroom door, caught his attention next. He eyed Kate. If she'd heard Caitlin, then she was clearly ignoring her. She simply lay there, laughing . . . laughing.

"Daddy?"

He turned, took a few steps, and looked out their bedroom door. Sure enough, standing in her yellow flowered nightgown at the end of their long hallway was his daughter—crying, rubbing her red, puffy eyes with small, closed fists.

She's had a nightmare. He walked toward her, Kate's laughter still sounding behind him.

He was within two feet of Caitlin when suddenly a thick steel wall slammed down from the ceiling, blocking his path to his daughter.

Scott was taken aback. The door looked just like one of the elevator doors at the station. *Where'd this come from?* He reached for a doorknob, but found nothing he could hold or grab; it was completely smooth. Over Kate's laughter, Scott thought he could hear thudding coming from beyond the steel wall. He placed his ear against it and could clearly make out the sound of his daughter's shrieking and squealing, pounding her little fists with all her might. "Let me in, Daddy! Let me in!"

"Dad!"

It was his twelve-year-old son's voice now. He was standing in a doorway at the other end of the hall. "Justin?" he called out, sprinting toward him. But again a steel panel slid into place, preventing him from reaching his son. His eyes darted back to the first steel door, and he noticed a small glass window through which he could see Caitlin crying, panicky, her face wet with tears. He hadn't noticed the window earlier. It was just high enough for Caitlin to look comfortably through . . . His eyes darted back to Justin's steel barrier. Sure enough, he now saw a window matching his boy's height. Justin, too, had a look of panic in his eyes, clearly terrified at not being able to get to his father. Scott found himself joining his boy as they pounded together against the seemingly impenetrable barrier. He could feel the hardness of the steel as he pounded ineffectually, but after only a few seconds noticed he didn't feel any pain. He wondered if his adrenaline numbed his skin too much for him to feel anything.

As his attention drifted from his frantic pounding back to Kate, he turned his head toward the bedroom. With a thud, a third wall of steel dropped in front of his own bedroom door a few feet to his left. In seconds he could hear the muffled sounds of Kate pounding against her own wall, pleading for help from the other side.

Scott's remaining daughter, Ashley, had apparently joined her twin sister at the end of the hall. Their voices now chorused in a consistent, agonizing plea for help—for his help.

Scott couldn't reach them to comfort them. His entire family was begging for his help . . . and he could do nothing! *I've lost them!* he thought to himself. *It's the changes! It has to be. I'm losing them!*

He ran up to Kate's steel wall. "Can you hear me?" he shouted through cupped hands, pressed against its surface.

Scott was about to call out again when he saw the small window, chin height, in the door—Kate's window. He glanced over his shoulder. Not only could he hear his family's pleading, but he could see each of their nearly hysterical faces as well.

Scott's hands moved quickly over Kate's barrier. It was smooth as well—no knobs or handles—and the bottom of it seemed to sink several inches into the carpet and wood of the floor. It was hopeless. He simply had no way to budge it.

He spun around as he heard a scraping metallic roar. Frozen in place, he watched the twins' barrier moving slowly in his direction—scraping against the walls, floor, and ceiling. Hanging photos and artwork crashed to the floor. Flecks of paint and wallboard showered toward him. The carpet began bunching up, as the steel wall plowed forward. Baseboards warped, pulling free from the wall, sending nails and splinters flying in all directions. Sparks showered the now-shifting floor as the steel wall scraped past the first light fixture.

The twins' faces, still visible, were moving with the wall, terrified as they continued to shout and plead for their father's help. The wall kept coming closer! Was it going to crush him?

He spun around and looked through the small window into his bedroom, his eyes finally locking with Kate's. Her face was pressed to the glass, and she was no longer screaming or pounding on the door. She was laughing again—laughing . . . at . . . *him*!

He turned away to find the steel wall moving closer, seemingly picking up speed.

Scott squeezed his eyes shut as it rushed at him, accepting the fact that he was going to be crushed—crushed into Kate's laughing image.

* * *

Scott awoke with a start, lying on nothing, surrounded by darkness. His breathing was labored as he fearfully looked about him.

"What . . . what—"

"It's all right," came the now-familiar voice of the guardian.

Fear ebbed into panic. "What's happening? What's going on?" he gasped, struggling to control his breathing. He didn't wait for an answer. He stood, turned around, and began walking—he could almost feel the steel door coming for him.

"Scott, you have to relax," the guardian assured him. "You've just had a dream."

He began jogging, moving faster, his mind struggling with the fact that he was running in total darkness. Surely he'd hit a wall—something.

Panic combined with frustration to turn Scott's jog into an eventual sprint. He was running with everything he had, his mind still screaming at him, warning him that he couldn't see *anything* in front of him.

Scott swallowed hard, his lungs working, taking in oxygen. *If I hit a wall,* he told himself, *I hit a wall. What difference does it make?*

After some time, though, it was clear that there would never be a wall. He slowed to a jog, eventually coming to a stop.

Dropping a hand to each knee, he bent over, gasping for air. Sweat streamed down his face, and the muscles in his legs were burning from the sudden strain. When he caught his breath, he straightened and looked all about him.

"Scott?" called the voice.

He couldn't answer the guardian. He just couldn't.

"Scott, it was the shock of seeing Kate. I never should have allowed it. As a defense mechanism, your mind disengaged itself temporarily from reality. But, Scott, remember what I told you. Sometimes a dream is just that—a dream."

And then, like a small, lost child, Scott sat . . . and began to cry.

CHAPTER 18

His knees pulled close to his chest, Scott sat with his arms locked around them, his eyes staring straight ahead, and the emptiness about him forgotten.

As disturbing as the dream had been, its details and the strength of the emotions he had felt were fading even now. It was the events that had obviously inspired it that still shook him.

Your children will never be.

For hours, it seemed, that statement reverberated within his mind.

How many times had he longed for peace and quiet, without the off-key sounds of a trumpet or piano finding their way under every door he closed, echoing through every heating vent in their house? How often had he wished for the chance to simply go somewhere without having to worry about the cost of a sitter, or waiting for a vacation that didn't interfere with school schedules? How many times had he wished for the chance to own something that wouldn't be discovered (no matter where he'd hidden it) and then broken or damaged "by accident"? Braces, clothes, and shoes—everything revolved around his children.

And now, in the solitude of this empty world, Scott realized that was exactly the way it was supposed to be. His son Justin and twin daughters Caitlin and Ashley were the center of his world. Their smiles and tears, hugs and kisses, made his life richer—gave it meaning and purpose. Sure, they could push his patience to the limit, but he also realized just how little patience he would have developed without them. Children had forced him to look outside himself, to learn the true meaning of love, and to grow. Without them, he felt empty and alone.

Scott looked beyond his knees into the blackness. *Empty and alone,* he repeated to himself.

Now, more than ever, he longed for one of their hugs, to see an innocent smile.

He let out a nervous chuckle. *I'd even accept crying at this point. Heck! Bring on the trumpet!*

Though nothing in his surroundings changed with these thoughts, Scott knew that *he* had. He also knew that when he did see his children again—at least he hoped he would see them again—he would try to remember what he'd learned. He'd been short with them in the past, but he could do better. He regretted some of the things he'd said and done over the years, but then, didn't most parents feel that way at times? *"All you can do is try your best, each and every day,"* his mother would often remind him, *"and hope you learn from your mistakes."*

He was learning, and hoped to one day be able to love his children and Kate all the more because of . . . whatever was happening.

But the more he pondered his resolution, the more tears came to his eyes. For as much as he wanted to use what he'd learned, he honestly wasn't sure if he ever could. What if these changes remained permanent? What if there was no way to get back what he once had? Had he truly sacrificed his family—shutting them away from him—for the fulfillment of a few selfish desires?

Despair and loneliness began to set in. The emptiness about him seemed cooler, and Scott hugged his legs to his chest even tighter. He no longer wanted to move forward in time, watching the consequences of his choices unfold. There seemed little point in it; those he loved with all of his heart were no longer a part of his life. Without them . . .

"Scott, it's time to move on."

The voice, though it had spoken suddenly, hadn't startled him. In fact, Scott was becoming so familiar with the guardian that he was beginning to sense the voice even before the words began, as if he could detect an intake of breath.

"Scott?" the guardian prompted.

"I really don't see the point," he answered quietly.

"But your life is only beginning, Scott. There is so much more to see."

"Perhaps to you it's beginning, but I don't really know that Scott anymore. Whatever path he's on hardly concerns me, don't you think?"

"You should see this through, Scott. After all, you are responsible for placing him on that path—"

"Look, I told you, I'm not interested in seeing any more. My wife is gone and so are my kids. Without them," he tightened his grip on his wrist, "I'm . . . nothing."

"Shall we move five or ten years into the future?" the guardian suggested implacably.

Scott grimaced. "Are you *deaf* or something? I said I'm not interested! What's so hard to understand about that? I'm done playing your games. I've had it! Now, if you don't mind, I'd like to be alone—" He cut himself off as the irony of the statement came home to him. "Just . . . be quiet," he finally concluded.

The voice didn't respond, which Scott took as a sign of acknowledgment, and he rested his forehead on his knees. He shook his head slowly. "Besides," he muttered, "what difference would five years make anyway?"

The faint sound of a crowd chanting was the first sign of a response from the guardian.

CHAPTER 19

Lifting his head, Scott found himself sitting in what appeared to be the same bedroom he'd ransacked earlier while looking for signs of a family. All was dark, except for a faint flickering light from the mansion's living room below. He identified it as the glow from a television set, bouncing and reflecting off the walls and ceiling before finding its way into the bedroom through the doorway and the large glass wall. Scott was seated on the floor at the foot of the enormous bed.

Scott closed his eyes and gave a cheerless grin. "Cute, Guardian," he mumbled. "Real cute." He raised his voice. "You're bound and determined to make me go through with this, aren't you? You won't be satisfied until you've ground me into the pavement." And then in an even louder voice he said, "Who's really calling the shots here, huh, Guardian? Who?"

There was no answer.

Scott resumed a normal tone of voice. "Well, just because I'm here doesn't mean I have to move. I'll just sit here until—"

A brown bottle slammed into the glass wall directly in front of him. The wall held, but the bottle shattered, showering the kitchen below with shards of debris.

"What the . . . ?" Scott jumped up, flinching seconds later when another bottle shattered against the wall just outside the bedroom doorway.

He heard a loud and heavy thud from below.

Curiosity overcame fear for his own safety. Cautiously Scott peered down from the edge of the doorway, trying to see into the

living room below, preferring the safety of the doorjamb to the
exposed glass wall.

He could see the wide-screen television, but nothing more from
this angle. *A football game,* he realized.

The hallway was dark and empty. He craned his head around the
doorjamb and peered into the living room below.

A fire was burning in the fireplace, and a quick glance outside the
room's large, open windows revealed several nearby trees, dusted with
snow, faintly lit under the pale wash of a near-full moon.

One of the hanging works of art caught his eye next, for it had obviously been the target of one of the bottles—a large piece of it swung
awkwardly, a substantial portion of its fragile frame broken by the blow.

Within the flickering orange light below, all was chaos. Couch
cushions had been ripped and thrown, bookcases overturned, and
several pieces of statuary lay crumbled at the base of the stone wall.
Was he was witnessing a robbery or . . . or what?

There was something between the couch and one of the coffee
tables. He squinted. It looked like a man—Scotty?—lying unconscious on the floor. Several bottles surrounded him, and the faint
smell of liquor was noticeable in the air.

"What's going on here, Guardian?"

No response.

Scott rolled his eyes and stepped out into the hallway, broken
glass crunching beneath his feet as he stood at the railing.

His eyes were inexplicably drawn to a manila folder on the floor
in front of the fireplace. Scott didn't bother asking the voice what the
folder contained; the guardian probably wouldn't tell him. But for
some strange reason, Scott felt the intense need to open it. Only after
a slight hesitation did he turn and make his way toward and then
down the wide, circular staircase.

He was startled by the grandfather clock's chiming as he reached
the ground floor. It read three o'clock, and it struck him as being odd
that a football game would be playing so early in the morning, but it
was clearly dark outside.

Entering the living room, he looked more closely at the television
screen and soon realized that the game was a recording—homemade
footage of a bowl game, he guessed, from Scott's—Scotty's—past.

He stepped over most of the debris, kicking aside a few throw pillows as he went. When he reached the coffee table, his foot bumped one of many bottles scattered on the floor.

Beer. "I take it I've left the Church," he commented aloud.

This time the voice replied. "You left the Church, Scott, after leaving home. Before that you had simply gone to church to please your mother. But important management meetings 'got in the way' afterward."

Stepping around the couch to reach the folder, he froze, shocked at what he saw.

On the floor, faceup with the eyes closed, was his body—pudgy and seemingly lifeless—appearing *ten* years older, rather than just five. *So much for the wonderful workout room,* he thought. Not only did his alternative self look disheveled and out of shape, but he smelled bad as well. It was clear from the looks of his clothes and unkempt hair that he hadn't bathed in several days. Scott glanced toward the dining room table and noticed it was covered with open pizza boxes and take-out food containers. It was obvious he hadn't left the house for days either.

His eyes returned once more to the body. It repulsed him. He felt an odd sort of detachment at seeing his own body. Despite the obvious resemblance, there were so many memories and experiences missing that Scott now felt little connection with the haggard form at his feet. Scotty was more a stranger now than an alter ego. That thought sent a chill up Scott's spine. He had almost nothing in common with this man, and he knew it.

Scott avoided the urge to turn on a light. The flickering light from the fire and the television was sufficient, and the low volume of the game overhead was now more a comfort than a distraction.

He spied the folder once more and finally walked over to the edge of the fireplace to pick it up. A few sheets of paper lay scattered on the floor beside it, and Scott wondered if Scotty had attempted to toss it into the fire.

He opened it and discovered that the folder contained several letters, each from a different corporation or business.

"What are these?" Scott asked.

"Cancellation notices," replied the voice, unnecessarily, as Scott was now reading the first letter. He skipped to the second paragraph.

We no longer require your services. He jumped to the end. *We appreciate all you have done for us in the past . . .* he stopped reading. "I don't get it."

He thumbed through a few of the others. Each said essentially the same thing.

"Your secretary delivered the folder. For the last month you've been away on an exotic cruise, leaving explicit instructions not to be disturbed. She felt her only alternative was to deliver these letters in person the day you got back. That was four days ago."

Scott was still confused. "That doesn't answer my question."

"Two weeks ago a new computer operating system was released—an upgrade to an existing one," began the guardian.

"Okay."

"In an effort to shore up their product sales, a few new features were included as part of the upgrade."

"Sure," said Scott. "Happens all the time."

"A virus utility, with free daily upgrades, was part of that package."

Suddenly the slight noise from the television overhead became a distraction again. Scott glanced at the body on the floor. "And so his company . . ."

"Provides a service that can now be had for free," finished the guardian.

Scott's head was spinning. "But surely they would have contracted out to other companies to service the software, to handle the maintenance required. They couldn't possibly handle all of that on their own. Not at first, anyway."

"They did, Scott. They're using two companies to handle the change—with sound business sense and experience—not your company."

"So then—"

"Scotty made a lot of money," the guardian said gently, "but he took the fast-track approach when it came to building his business. He just didn't have what it took to efficiently handle it, Scott. He didn't even have a degree, remember? He was in over his head, and to potential investors, it showed."

Scott closed the folder. "So he's lost everything?"

"As impressive as this mansion might seem, and as rich as Scotty might appear on the outside, it's all an illusion. He had no discipline when it came to money matters. And since he has no liquid assets to speak of, without a business to provide a steady stream of cash, all of this . . . disappears."

Scott shook his head, unsure of how he was supposed to feel. "Did he ever marry?"

"Twice," replied the guardian. "Each marriage lasted less than a year. He just couldn't seem to commit himself to any kind of permanent relationship."

"Children?"

"No."

"Good." He tossed the folder into the fire and watched as it flared. "Companies fold all the time. I'm sure his employees will move on. At least he's . . . *I'm*, the only one hurt by all this. I'm the only one that will really lose anything."

"Well, this isn't the only house you had, Scott."

His brow furrowed. "What, I had a summer home in Paris?" he asked sarcastically. He hooked a thumb over his shoulder at the body on the floor. "It's doubtful I'd be selfless enough to buy anyone a home."

"But you did, Scott."

"For whom?" he asked skeptically. The guardian was silent. Then it dawned on him. "Mom?" He felt his stomach drop.

"She fought you on it for months, but eventually caved in," the guardian confirmed. "You convinced her that she deserved something more than what she had, though her home had been completely paid for after your father's death. When she finally relented, you were as pleased as could be. *She* got what you felt she deserved, and *you* got what you'd been looking for all along. It helped ease your conscience over areas in which you knew you'd fallen short in your mother's eyes."

Scott shut his eyes, now ashamed he'd simply tossed aside the losses of countless employees earlier. Of course others would suffer. Why wouldn't they? Including those *indirectly* linked to the company, like his mother.

Slowly he began to shake his head. "But . . . how could things have turned out so bad? I always listened to my heart when it came to making decisions. Okay, we don't share the same interests now, and he hasn't had the same schooling that I've had, but . . . but he has the same heart . . . deep down."

"And he used to listen to that heart, Scott. But from an early age he stopped doing that."

"What do you mean?" Scott asked quietly, staring into the fire.

"Instead of listening to his heart," explained the guardian, "he's been listening . . . to you."

He turned in despair to stare at Scotty's form once more . . . but was shocked to find the body no longer lying on the floor. Rather, Scotty was now standing, a large metal figurine raised high above his head.

"Stop!" Scott yelled. With the fire at his back he had nowhere to go. "It's me, Scotty!"

Scotty hesitated. Scruffy and bleary-eyed, he squinted his eyes. "You?"

In an instant, recognition and then rage flared from his bloodshot eyes, his lips curling into an ugly snarl. "You!" And then he began to laugh, lowering his arm and taking a few steps backward. His laughter only lasted a few seconds before suddenly turning into a hacking cough.

Scott stood still, simply watching, not knowing what to say or do.

Wiping his hand over his whiskered chin, Scotty began to mumble. He was clearly drunk, but, after mumbling several lines of unintelligible nonsense, his words became more audible, though still slurred. "I . . . I'd make millions, you said. You . . . said I'd be wealthy. You said I'd never . . ." he swallowed. "You said I'd never have to worry about . . . money again." He took a deep breath before yelling, "You liar!"

He spat, the putrid spittle hitting Scott directly in the face.

Scott wiped at his eyes to clear them . . . and the first thing he saw when he pulled his hand from his face was the raised figurine again racing toward his head.

Scott's cry for the guardian never made it past his lips.

CHAPTER 20

Scott's eyes slammed shut, his hands flying above his head to protect himself against . . . against a blow that never came.

He'd been pulled once more into the empty, black realm of nothing.

He bent over, his hands dropping to his knees as he struggled to regain control of his breathing, his heart pounding in protest.

Scott opened his eyes.

As difficult as it was to overcome the shock of what he'd just experienced, equally difficult was keeping at bay the anger rising within. But after all, the guardian could have let him experience the full impact of the figurine and Scott was grateful that he hadn't.

"Scott, please understand," the guardian began. "I haven't enjoyed putting you though all of this—"

"If it's been so blasted difficult," interrupted Scott as he straightened, his jaw clenched, "then why do it?"

"It was necessary for you to truly understand the impact your decisions have had on your life."

"Yeah? Well, enough already. Enough! I get the point. My decisions were poor ones. I get it! I . . . I get it."

But Scott still didn't understand and for several minutes he paced, trying to make sense of his emotions.

"It's just . . ." He stopped and ran his hands through his hair, frustrated.

"It's just what, Scott?"

Scott sat down, pulling his knees into his body once more. "Forget it. Let's just . . . forget it."

"Please, Scott. I want to help."

Scott let out a nervous laugh. "You really think I'm just going to open up to you? You're out of your mind. Before I know it you'll have me climbing Arctic glaciers, making me watch as I *find myself*. No thanks." His mouth twisted in a bitter smile at that thought.

"Please, Guardian. No more traveling . . . okay?" asked Scott. "I don't think . . . I could handle any more. Please?"

"That's all right, Scott. We're through traveling, if that is your wish. I promise you that. No more."

Scott nodded silently, grateful.

"Now, what were you going to say?" prompted the guardian.

It took a moment for Scott to pull himself together, to come up with words to express his confusion.

"What was . . ." he began, but stopped, wiping his eyes with the heels of his hands.

"Go on, Scott. Just say what comes to mind. I want to help."

Scott let out the breath he hadn't realized he'd been holding. Was the guardian really there to help him, or was he just there to torture him? How could he know for certain that the voice wouldn't suddenly turn on him . . .

No. I don't think he would, Scott finally concluded. *He . . . seems sincere,* he thought. Several more minutes passed in silence, and Scott finally decided he had nothing to lose. He'd just have to trust the voice, and if it turned on him and threw him someplace unexpected, then he'd deal with it. What choice did he really have?

"I can see how badly everything's turned out. But, for crying out loud, what was so wrong with what I did?" he finally asked. "I mean, seriously!" Scott chose his next words carefully. "The first thing I did was what? Help Scotty stand up for himself, not allow himself to be pushed around by bullies? You're telling me that standing up for yourself is wrong?"

"Of course not, Scott."

"And . . . what's wrong with having more friends? A wider circle of friends—to do things with."

"Nothing at all," the guardian agreed.

Scott gave a curt nod and stood, beginning to pace once more.

"Sports have done wonders for Justin," Scott pointed out after much thought. "If it hadn't been for soccer, I don't know where his self-esteem would be right now. He thrives on it, and has made some very good friends."

"You're right. It has helped Justin."

"And I know *many* wealthy people who do *great* things with what they have. They have solid marriages and lead very productive lives—philanthropists. That's what the world calls them, because they give and give and give."

"That's true," the guardian replied.

Scott stopped pacing—a bit confused at all the agreement he was receiving. "So why is it, if I'm so right, that *I* can't have any of that?"

For nearly a minute there was silence. And then the guardian began to speak: "Scott, to begin with, tell me what really happened that day when Jerry and his friends confronted you?"

"Oh, come on." Scott was genuinely frustrated. "We're not going to go through all that again—"

"You've asked the questions, Scott. Please, give me the chance to answer them."

Scott released a huge sigh. "All right. Sure."

The guardian began again. "Thank you. I need you to answer my question first, Scott. What really happened that day? To you, not to Scotty after you spoke to him."

"Surely you know—"

"Scott," the guardian warned.

"All right! Fine." Scott sat, clasping his hands around his bent legs once more.

After taking a moment to collect his thoughts, he began. "They stopped and hassled me for several minutes, and Jerry *did* punch me four times. That's . . . that's when I realized his punches didn't hurt as bad as I thought they would."

"And?" prompted the guardian.

"And . . . so I went for him, swinging. I was furious, fed up with all the teasing. Something inside of me just snapped." Scott grimaced and shook his head. "But my punches were all wild. None of them made contact."

"And then Jerry's mother drove by."

Scott's head dropped at the memory. "Yeah."

"And when you saw her, you stopped swinging. Why, Scott?"

This time it was Scott's turn to remain silent.

The voice finished Scott's thought for him. "You remembered at that moment something your mother had told you several times before, didn't you?"

Scott nodded slowly. He cleared his throat. "She often reminded me that . . ." Scott fell silent.

"Please go on, Scott. I assure you I wouldn't be asking you about this if it wasn't necessary to answer your question. You can trust me."

Scott simply nodded, sincerely hoping his trust wasn't misplaced. "She often reminded me that Jerry'd had a rough life."

"How so?"

"I . . . I guess his father left him and his mother and sister when Jerry was really young."

"Young, but old enough to remember," added the voice.

"I guess so. Mom said that even though I'd lost *my* father, at least we'd had some quality time together. Jerry hadn't had any, really."

"And your father had provided well for you even after his death—investments, insurance . . . Jerry's mother had none of that."

"I suppose. 'He's bitter,' she used to say. 'But try and understand where it comes from.'"

"But the teasing still hurt, didn't it?" the guardian asked.

Again, he nodded. "Yeah, it did."

"And, yet, when you saw you had the chance to clobber him, even with the wild punches, you stopped and walked away."

Scott sighed once more.

"Why, Scott?" asked the guardian.

"After I saw his mother's face, her eyes . . . you're right. I knew I had it in me to pound him, to get even. I knew it. Given another few seconds I would have worked past the adrenaline. But when I saw her . . ." he trailed off.

"Go on, Scott," the guardian prompted.

"I . . . could imagine her hugging him later . . . later that evening . . . consoling him, struggling to deal with . . . with yet another *bad* card in what was already, for her, a *bad* hand. And I . . . I just couldn't go through with it."

"And did the teasing stop afterward?" asked the guardian.

Scott grinned. "Jerry backed off a bit." And then he frowned and his voice grew louder. "But his friends didn't. They broke the clay heart and—"

"Scott, I think you're missing the point."

"What? I—"

"Scott, you *did* stand up to Jerry, and you *did* teach him that you couldn't be pushed around. *He* saw the rage in your eyes. The others didn't."

"Yes, but they—"

"Scott, think about it," interrupted the guardian. "You eventually formed a truce with each of them, didn't you? It took a few years with some of them, but the teasing didn't last forever."

"But—"

"Did it?" the guardian stopped him.

When the answer came it was in a quiet whisper. "No."

"Eventually you learned how to overcome their comments with humor. You never became best friends, but an understanding developed. Didn't it?"

Scott simply sat there, reflecting back on each of the guys who had caused him trouble. The guardian was right. He *had* found ways to cope with each one of them.

"Scott, for years you have associated weakness with your run-ins with Jerry. But it wasn't weakness you were exercising that particular day, it was compassion. Your mother taught you to consider situations from the other person's perspective, not just your own."

After a momentary pause, the guardian added, "It has never been your weakness, Scott. It's been your strength."

Scott was stunned. He'd never looked at it from that angle before. After a moment of thought though, he was still confused. "But surely that one event wouldn't have completely undone what Mom had taught me," he pointed out.

"Scott, compassion demands patience and long-suffering. You know that. With your help, Scotty saw in an instant just how quickly he was able to change his situation with his fists; the results were nearly instantaneous. On a young and impressionable mind, which outcome is going to appear more desirable—the unseen road of patience and a few hard knocks, or the instant results found with a balled fist and a forceful personality?"

The question was a rhetorical one, and Scott saw little point in answering it.

"Your reaction to Jerry that day may have been justified, and would have served its purpose, but Scotty took it too far."

Scott couldn't help wincing at the memory of just *how* far Scotty had taken it.

The guardian continued. "Compassion breeds incredible opportunities, but it is a tender virtue and must be nurtured with care. Scotty found a faster solution to his problem on the day of your visit. What budding compassion had existed then withered away."

Scott was silent.

"Now, concerning your second question. Of course there's nothing wrong with having lots of friends. But having the right kind of friends, Scott, matters more than the sheer number of them. You had *many* friends, if you look back with an honest perspective. But what kind of friends did you have? They weren't the kind that partied or schmoozed with the more popular kids, or adults. They were more than that."

"What do you mean?" Scott asked quietly.

"Throughout your life your friends have uplifted, helped, and inspired you. They still do. Think about it, Scott. Am I right?"

Scott again nodded slowly. The guardian *was* right. They might not have been the most popular people, but they *had* been there for him. They'd always been there for him.

"And as far as sports are concerned, they can be very beneficial . . . for the right personality. For Justin, it works. The combination is a natural. In fact, remember Sanchez from high school? Sports was his social life-preserver. It gave him direction, something in common with those around him, and helped to produce a very well-rounded, bright young man. But with you, it wouldn't have had the same effect. It just wasn't what you needed."

The guardian hardly paused. "And money? Scott, one day you might have more than you need. But when you do, you'll know how to manage it because of all the budgeting you're forced to do now."

"But a little bigger home—" Scott objected.

The guardian interrupted him. "Doesn't yours keep you warm enough? Scott, you want more for your family. That's natural. But as you've already seen, sometimes more, in reality, is less."

It was silent for some time as Scott pondered the guardian's words and the perspective they offered.

The voice was the first to break the silence. "Scott, you do a lot of good doing what you do."

Scott thought the tone was meant to be reassuring, but he couldn't help laughing out loud. "Please! I sell advertising space for a third-rate radio station. I hardly believe that qualifies as making the world a better place."

"Scott, it's not the job you have that matters, but how you treat those around you that counts. Again, the compassion you've developed over the years has proven effective in your dealings with clients and co-workers. Hasn't it?

"Your clients know they can trust you, know you'll listen to their concerns and truly strive to understand their point of view. And the owners, manager, and sales manager know you can be trusted. They know you'd never falsify affidavits, and trust they will be well represented by you in the community.

"Besides . . ." Scott thought he could once more detect a hint of amusement in the voice. "You like what you do, don't you?"

Reluctantly, Scott nodded. Sure, quotas had to be met and there were always the tensions that existed between Programming and Sales, but overall he *did* enjoy his job. The satisfaction of achieving monthly goals and pleasing clients was rewarding. And while it was true that he did live in a relatively small area, naturally limiting his client potential, the community was proving ideal to raise a family in.

Many of his co-workers had told him they could easily see him becoming station manager one day. Perhaps he would. But, for now, he was happy simply being an account executive—nothing more.

And after seeing that Kate truly wouldn't have had life any other way, he was beginning to realize that life wasn't nearly as bleak as he'd thought earlier.

Bleak? wondered Scott. *When did I think life was bleak?*

"All of us go through life at the pace that's right for us, Scott. It's when we become impatient, and interfere with that pace, that we fall into trouble."

Scott heard the guardian's words, but was focusing more on his last thought. *When did I think my life was . . . bleak?*

The guardian continued, "You wondered earlier how one simple action could effect so much change. It's no different from a car traveling at a considerable speed, really. A quarter-inch nudge on the steering wheel might not seem like much at first, but in the long run—weeks or even months later—your destination will have been altered greatly, placing you miles from your intended goal. Does that make sense, Scott?"

Scott didn't answer . . . *Car? . . . Bleak?*

"What is it, Scott?" the guardian finally seemed to notice that Scott wasn't listening to him.

The dashboard of his van flashed through Scott's mind. The red glow of an engine light.

"The van," Scott said vaguely.

"What about it?"

Scott remembered hitting a steering wheel with his fist.

"The alternator! It went . . . just like I was afraid it would," Scott said more firmly.

"What are you talking about?" Scott couldn't tell if the guardian was truly confused, or if he was being disingenuous.

He struggled to keep his own emotions under control. For the first time since he'd been here, he realized he was beginning to remember something more than distant memories. He might even be beginning to piece together what had led up to his being here.

"The . . . the alternator went!" he repeated with excitement in his voice. "I remember being upset. It was just after Halloween— Thanksgiving and Christmas were just around the corner. Money was tight . . . bills . . .

"Halloween! October!" he shouted excitedly. "I *knew* I was right about the odd weather here . . . there . . . you know what I mean."

"What else do you remember, Scott?" the guardian sounded genuinely curious this time.

Scott shut his eyes. He was now sitting cross-legged, and he gripped his knees, struggling to remember.

"Rain—cold rain. It was raining, hard! I was driving slowly. I was on my way to have the alternator checked after work, but the slow speed, the heater, the defrost, the extra time it was taking me . . . it must have drained it—"

Cold, wet feet—his feet—flashed through Scott's mind. "Walking . . . I got out to walk." He said decisively. "I decided to walk toward a . . . a house. Yes, a house—in the distance!" Scott was excited, for the memories seemed to be coming easier now. "I rounded a bend in the road," he continued. "A guardrail. There was a guardrail and . . ."

"Yes, Scott?" the guardian prompted.

His excitement began to fade, and he felt a cold and anxious feeling begin to flow through his veins . . . out to his hands and feet. He realized they felt numb. Then he drew in his breath sharply.

"Headlights!" Scott shouted.

"Where?" asked the guardian calmly.

"Behind me! A car going too fast! It . . . it can't see me in the rain!" Sweat broke out on Scott's forehead and his breathing became labored, his words now short and forced.

"Can't . . . see. Too fast. It's coming too fast! Sliding . . . no! . . . It's . . . going to . . . going to . . ."

"It's going to what, Scott?"

"Hit me!" He frantically stood, looked about him, and shook his head—all his excitement at remembering was forgotten.

"No. No!"

"Scott, you must listen to me now."

"It can't be," muttered Scott, shaking his head and wringing his hands. "It just can't be!"

"Scott—"

Scott looked helplessly into the empty darkness. "I'm dead!"

CHAPTER 21

"Scott, can you hear me? I love you, Scott. Please come back. I love you . . ."

* * *

"Easy, Scott," came the guardian's voice. "Relax. You're not dead. Although you almost slipped from reality again. You just need to relax and listen to me."

Scott felt as if he were coming out of a daze. "But I don't eat," he babbled. "I don't have to shave, I . . ." He turned, his arms extended, gesturing at the blackness. "Look at where I am!"

"Scott, if you'll just—"

"Then there's you!" interrupted Scott. "Who—what—are you?"

"Scott, re—"

"Don't tell me to relax! It's easy for you. You have all the answers! You know *exactly* what's going on. I'm . . . I'm in the dark. Literally!"

"All right, Scott. I understand what you must be feeling right now, but if you'll calm down, I'll tell you exactly what's happened. Have a seat, and I promise to tell you everything."

Scott considered the guardian's words carefully. "No tricks?" he asked suspiciously. "I told you, I don't think I can handle—"

The guardian cut him off, "No tricks, Scott. I give you my word. We will only talk."

Scott took a deep breath and attempted to gain control over his emotions, but he found it difficult. He did want answers. Though, as he sat, instinctively pulling his knees into his body and hugging them once more, a part of him was now becoming fearful of what he would discover.

"Go ahead," he said finally. "I'm listening. But please, no riddles, no proverbs—just give it to me straight."

"Of course, Scott. To begin with, you were right. Your van stalled and you managed to get it over to the side of the road. You knew the chances of anyone seeing you in a storm like this were slim, and you were also concerned about sitting there all night and freezing. And the van's battery would only power the lights for so long."

"A house," interjected Scott.

"That's right. You thought you could make out a porch light in the distance and decided to risk it. If you could find a house, then you could call for help. It was very cold and the rain was coming down hard enough to make it difficult to see. You were soaked in a matter of seconds, and . . . an approaching car *did* hit you."

"So, I'm dead," Scott concluded in exasperation.

"No, Scott," answered the guardian. Scott sensed a great deal of sympathy in those words. "It was only the back end of the car that clipped you, sending you into the guardrail. Had it hit you head-on, or followed you into the rail, you would have been killed instantly."

Scott was still confused. He remembered flashes of everything the voice had described. But they were just that—flashes and snippets of memory. Had the voice not put all of them together, he doubted if he would have ever made sense of them in his current situation. But it was his *current* situation that put all the pieces being assembled into question. If he'd been in a wreck . . . what was he doing here? Shouldn't he be home? In a hospital? Lying in wet dirt and grass? He tried to remain patient. "So what happened?" he prodded.

"You were badly broken up. The woman from the car that hit you, and a truck driver, both helped to stop a lot of the bleeding. The woman called for help. Without their help, you wouldn't have had much of a chance in that storm with the temperature dropping the way it was."

"But—"

"You're in a coma, Scott," the guardian finally revealed flatly.

The voice then fell silent, giving Scott time to absorb this new revelation.

"I'm . . . in a coma?"

"Yes. There's a blood clot in your brain. It's inoperable. They were hoping it would be absorbed fairly quickly by your body, although there's still no guarantee about how much brain damage it will leave."

Scott was perplexed. He struggled to even open his mouth, the words forming slowly around his tongue. "Right now, I'm . . . in a hospital . . . in a coma?"

"That's right. The blood clot has not dissolved as quickly as the doctors had hoped, and you are still unconscious."

Scott was dumbfounded. He turned the idea over in his mind. Was that it, then? Was he nothing more than a prisoner in his own mind—a victim of his own subconscious?

He looked down at his hands, clenching them into fists, and then rubbed his palms over his knees and legs. He simply couldn't believe it. "But I don't understand. How come everything seems so—" His head shot up. "You said this wasn't a dream," he accused.

"That's correct, Scott. It isn't a dream."

"But if I'm in a coma, this must be a dream," Scott said in triumph. "You're just part of my subconscious. You can't tell me this isn't a dream."

Scott thought he heard a sigh from the guardian. "Scott, this past year and a half has been very difficult for you and Kate." Here the guardian paused. Scott just waited, silently. "Even I'm not sure how much you will remember of the months leading up to the accident, due to your possible brain damage, although I'm encouraged by your memories of the accident so far. So bear with me if I repeat anything you already know." The guardian paused again. "For a time it looked as if you were finally going to score some high-profile contracts for the station—everything was exploding. The dot-com market was pumping millions of dollars into advertising, targeting big and small cities alike.

"And then the bubble burst. The downturn in the economy forced many into bankruptcy or tremendous downsizing. Ads and contracts were being cancelled left and right, causing profitability to plummet. And it wasn't long before all the extra money coming in had suddenly been cut off. With every verbal and nonverbal agreement that was cancelled, the dreams your small station had of expanding and growing became ever more distant.

"It wasn't long before you found yourself struggling to retain even your regular clients. It's been very stressful for you. And when you lost even a few of the regulars because of your unwillingness to 'bend the rules' . . . Well, you'd lost contracts before, but never like this. And with Thanksgiving and Christmas coming up, it hit you pretty hard. Medical and dental bills had also begun to pile up. All of you would have to tighten your belts, and Christmas . . . would have to be kept 'simple' this year. All of this was taking its toll on you," the guardian concluded. "The alternator, well—"

"Pushed me over the edge," finished Scott. It seemed like ages ago to him. "I remember." Everything was coming back in a rush: the pink slips, layoffs, lost contracts, Sky's unrelenting verbal jabs, delinquency notices in the mail and on the telephone. He had managed to hang on to his job, and to keep Sky Remington and his out-of-this-world plans at bay. He had been looking into a second, even a third job to help take up the slack once the unpaid bills began piling up. Kate had even started using some of their food storage . . .

"Often in your life when you've been depressed," the guardian began, "you've been able to bounce right back. But this time . . ."

Scott was gradually putting the picture into focus. "And the three things I changed . . ."

"They're the regrets you've always associated as being the underlying cause of almost every misfortune you've ever had. In the back of your mind, being more forceful, more popular, and having more money have always been the missing pieces needed to fill the perceived voids in your life. Scott, you needed to see that this was not the case. The accident—your coma—provided the ideal opportunity to reveal this to you."

"Reveal?" Scott whispered. "I . . . I don't understand."

"Scott, this is much more than a dream. You've been blessed with what you might call a vision."

Scott wondered vaguely how he could feel such a physical sense of shock if his body was in a coma. But it was no more surprising than any of the other things he had experienced. "A . . . vision?" he said slowly.

"A vision," confirmed the guardian. "You seemed to have forgotten that your life is a product of following your heart, and that your heart is in tune with the Lord's plan for you."

Scott, struggling to recover from his shock, felt a steadying sense of warmth entering his chest. He recognized that feeling; he realized it was the Spirit bearing witness to the truth. His eyes began to fill with tears. "But I thought visions were for prophetic warnings or to foretell things. If this isn't my future I've been experiencing, then . . ."

"Visions may also be given to teach truths. Visions are the fruit of faith. When a man follows his heart, Scott—follows the Spirit's lead—he'll never find himself where he shouldn't be. We might sometimes view a particular situation or event as impossible to overcome, when in reality it is precisely what we need in order to develop and grow."

Scott once again found his eyes drawn to his hands. He flexed his fingers once more. "It all seems so real."

"In a vision, all of your senses can be employed, allowing the message to become tangible and real. In this reality, you've been given the opportunity to see what would happen if you relied only on your own wisdom and understanding. While Scotty did appear more successful, appeared much better off, without the Lord's approval or backing, his sandy foundation couldn't withstand the buffetings of the world."

The voice subsided into silence for a time, apparently giving Scott the opportunity to take in all that he'd been told. Scott finally spoke. "So all my mistakes and failures and weaknesses—things that were disappointments in my life—not all of them were wrong choices or . . . or . . ."

Scott swiped at sudden tears as the voice clarified for him. "Yes, Scott, we all make mistakes, and some of your choices were mistakes and some weren't. But, in both cases, you seemed to have forgotten the Atonement. You weren't handing your burdens to the right person."

Scott nodded in silence.

"Scott, we all fall short at times, but understand that we are the sum total of our successes *and* failures. Tug on the thread of one and it loosens another. Remove those threads and, as you've seen, the tapestry of who you are eventually unravels . . . and falls apart."

After another long moment of silence, Scott finally found the heart to speak. "Then . . . the ultimate gift you mentioned at first . . . wasn't getting everything I wished for. The ultimate gift is . . . is to put me back on track in terms of . . . recognizing the Atonement. The gift is the Atonement."

"That's right, Scott. It always has been."

Silence prevailed.

"I've been selfish, haven't I?" Scott asked finally.

"In the past, and these past few months especially, you've been comparing your life to the lives of others. And you can't do that, Scott. You have your own life to live, with its own meaning and purpose. When you start comparing yourself to others, that's when jealously and depression creep in. And jealousy is a bottomless pit that can never be filled or satisfied, Scott. On the other hand, faith in Christ, which naturally leads to faith in His plan for us, brings with it a different result. 'But whosoever drinketh of the water that I shall give him shall never thirst; but the water that I shall give him shall be in him a well of water springing up into everlasting life.' That is His promise, Scott."

Scott sat silent, pondering all he had seen and heard—and learned.

The voice was right. He *had* been hard on himself lately. He'd been looking so hard at himself that he had lost sight of all he had around him—his blessings clouded and forgotten.

The sewing machine from the Gutierrez home in Guatemala suddenly came to mind. For all that shack wasn't, it was their home. And it was enough. He shook his head. *How dare I complain? How dare I ignore the gift that loosens my burdens so I can look to helping others?*

Scott's thoughts turned then to his own family. He had been blessed with a beautiful, caring wife, and three very dear children. He had a good job. And if it didn't pay enough, then he'd get another one, just as his father had done. And perhaps there were areas of his budget he could cut back on.

But he had a *good* life; it was full, and he was surrounded by people he cared deeply for, and who cared as much about him. After seeing what *could* have been, how empty his life *might* have become, he couldn't help appreciating more what he did have—problems and all. He didn't need everything he *thought* he needed.

After several minutes Scott cleared his throat and asked, "How long have I . . . been in this . . . coma?"

"A little over four months," replied the guardian simply.

Scott was shocked. He'd been completely unprepared for that answer. *Four months!* he thought to himself in amazement. It felt like it had been only a day or two. But Scott accepted the answer without argument.

I missed Christmas, he realized next. That troubled him even more than the fact he was in a coma.

"Christmas," Scott said softly, "must have been difficult for Kate and the kids."

"It was. But they're strong, Scott. It's only a holiday, and they understand that. You mean far more to them than any mere holiday."

Scott nodded, not quite sure how to take that answer.

He digested these revelations in silence. Finally he asked, "Can I go back?" He wanted the chance to apply everything he had learned. He wanted to ease some of the tension he'd allowed to enter his home lately. He wanted a second chance.

"That's not for me to decide, Scott," replied the guardian.

Again, Scott only nodded without arguing. He thought some more.

After several minutes Scott did the only thing he could think of doing. He slowly got to his knees and opened his heart to the Lord.

When Scott had closed his prayer and sat once more, drying his eyes, he was feeling more at peace than he had for quite some time.

"You've learned a lot, haven't you, Scott?"

The question was definitely an understatement. Scott gave a short laugh. "At least I know I haven't been sent to outer darkness. The thought *did* cross my mind, you know."

"Yes, I had a feeling it had." Once again, Scott thought he detected a smile amidst the words.

"Uh, Guardian? Look, I . . . I'm sorry if I've been short with you. You've been a great help to me, and I . . ."

"Thank someone else, Scott. Spend a little more time on your knees in gratitude. Things will work out."

Scott nodded once more, pondering all he had learned—all he had been reminded of.

After several minutes, the voice interrupted his thoughts. "You haven't asked me *when* you'll return, Scott. Aren't you the least bit curious?"

Scott smiled, his mind at peace. "I'll leave that in the Lord's hands. I can wait."

"Well done, my son. I'm pleased."

At this, Scott's eyes widened and his heart began to race. Until that very moment, the voice had been unrecognizable. Could it be . . . ?

"Dad? Dad, is that you?"

"Tell your mother I love her too, son."

CHAPTER 22

Scott slowly opened his eyes. He noticed Kate first. Her face lay buried in his shoulder, her long, auburn hair tickling his cheek from the shaking of her silent sobs.

"Kate?" he whispered softly past dry lips.

The shaking continued.

"Kate?" he managed, louder this time. The shaking stopped.

Cautiously, Kate raised her head—her eyes swollen and filled with tears. She blinked quickly, as if to make sure that her bleary-eyed vision wasn't playing tricks on her. But when she saw Scott's open eyes and the soft smile beginning to form on his face, her breath caught.

"I missed you," he said softly.

With that, Kate grabbed his left hand and held it close to their faces as she kissed his cheek and held her forehead next to his, her tears—now of joy—mixing with Scott's as she murmured, "I knew you'd come back! I knew it."

Scott was just as overjoyed at seeing his wife once more. He noticed next the sights, sounds, and smells of a hospital room. He hated hospitals—had ever since he was a child. But he took comfort in seeing everything tidy and in order—under control, it seemed.

A quick downward glance assured him that he was still in one piece, though he felt extremely weak. His feet, he saw, were flat against a board at the foot of the bed. And his right hand . . . He lifted it so he could examine it more closely.

Kate noticed him taking inventory. "A car hit you, Scott," she explained. "You were thrown into a guardrail. Your leg was broken in three places. You broke a few ribs on your left side and had a pretty

severe concussion. And your right hand was pretty banged up too."
Scott was still staring at the scars around his knuckles, the skin pink
and tender. "You've really healed well. The doctors have been hopeful
that . . ." She broke into tears once more.

He turned to her and brought her head back to his shoulder. "It's
okay, Kate," he reassured her. "Everything's going to be all right."

Both lay lost in their own thoughts, and Scott's eyes drifted once
more to his right hand. The broken bathroom mirror from the airport
flashed through his mind. "How long was I in casts?"

"About . . . about two months." Kate was searching his face, his
eyes. "How do you feel, Scott?"

He grinned. "Like a million dollars—cashier's check, of course.
Hopefully, I'll be able to cash it soon."

Kate didn't even smile at his dry remark. Her eyes continued to
search his face. Was she looking for something?

"What is it, Kate?"

She caught herself and quickly looked away from him. "I'm sorry,
Scott. It's just that . . ."

"What, sweetheart?"

She took a few seconds to collect herself and then began again.
"The doctors kept telling me that . . . that the longer you were out,
the greater the extent of . . ."

"Of what?"

"Brain damage," she answered finally.

He grinned. "Great. I can just hear your dad now." She didn't
seem to catch the humor in the remark and he weakly gave her hand
a squeeze. "It's okay, Kate. As far as I can tell, I'm just fine."

Relief washed over her face. "Besides," he continued, "the nice
part about brain damage is that you're the last one to know about it,
right? I love you, Tracy."

She gave his shoulder a light punch. "That's not funny." She
leaned in close to him once more.

Over her shoulder, Scott found his right, scarred hand, and for a
second wondered if everything he'd experienced—the voice, the dark
nothingness . . . the whole vision—had, in fact, really happened, or if
it had all been just a dream after all. But, seconds later, a smile
emerged; deep in his heart he knew it *had* been real. He had no

rational way of explaining *how* it had happened, but he just knew that it had. He felt it in his gut.

"Where are the kids, honey?"

Kate sat up, brushing her hair over her shoulder with her free hand, and swiped at her eyes. "They come by every other day after school. Your mom brings them over. She's been such a help, Scott." She glanced at the clock on the wall behind her. "They should be here any minute." She patted his hand. "I should tell the nurse you're awake."

She started to get up, but Scott kept his hold on her hand. "Hold on, Kate," he said softly. "Just sit with me a minute more, will you?" He smiled at her worried expression. "I'm okay. Really. Tired, but okay. I . . . I just want to sit with you a while. All right? I don't . . . I don't want to be left alone."

Her face softened and she raised and kissed his hand. "All right."

She's so beautiful, he thought, admiring her anew. He was happy and relieved to see the sparkle in her eye that had been missing earlier, when he'd seen her with—

"Have you noticed the flowers?" Kate asked, a welcome interruption to his thoughts.

"What?"

"The flowers," she repeated, pointedly glancing around the room. There were dozens of flower bouquets wrapped in colored foil lining the sink and the small windowsill across the room, as well as filling the corners of the small room.

Kate laughed at Scott's expression. "There are even more behind you."

Scott didn't dare crane his neck. "It's like a garden in here. Where did they come from?"

"Oh, Scott. You wouldn't believe the outpouring of support I've—*we've*—had. They're from co-workers, clients, people from church, neighbors, even the teachers from the kids' school. Everyone's been so thoughtful. I thought after the first week the flowers would stop, but . . ."

Her tears began once more, turning Scott's attention from the flowers to her. "Your clients . . . our friends . . ." She swallowed. "They wanted you to have fresh flowers when you woke up." Her eyes brightened.

"They've been wonderful, Scott. I never realized how many people have gotten to know you over the years."

Scott nodded silently, his gratitude making each brightly colored flower appear more and more beautiful by the minute.

"They . . . love you, Scott . . . and—" She wiped her eyes with her hand.

Scott gave her hand a squeeze. Tears were now rolling down his own cheeks as well. Kate continued. "The ward has also been a great help. At first I told Bishop Baker that I was embarrassed by all of the meals and . . . gifts. But he reminded me we need to let people give when they feel the need to. He . . ." she let out a short laugh. "He said your accident may have been a blessing in some ways—allowing others the chance to give and serve."

Kate's eyes dropped toward the floor, any humor in her face disappearing. "I got mad at him when he said that. The idea of others learning service at your expense . . . I'm selfish, I guess—Oh," she continued, "Chad told me to tell you the minute you woke up not to worry about a thing at work. He and a few others have been covering for you." She smiled. "He also wanted me to tell you to heal fast, before management figures out how 'expendable' you are." She gave his hand another squeeze. "He's kidding, of course. They've missed you. He also tells me that Sky's been eating a lot of humble pie lately." The smile on her face had turned smug.

"What do you mean?" asked Scott.

"A lot of the bigger clients he'd hooked up with have suffered some pretty hefty losses over the last few months. This recession's touched everyone. If it wasn't for the very clients Sky's always been putting down, Chad doubts they'd still have a station to run. Chad told me to tell you that you were right and that he's never going to doubt you again."

Kate moved in for another hug, overwhelmed again with emotion as Scott considered her words.

"The bishop's right, sweetheart," Scott finally whispered into her ear. He smiled. "There's more to all of this than either one of us realizes. Don't be too hard on him. I'm sure he was just trying to help you look beyond the problem—beyond yourself."

Kate nodded silently against his shoulder.

A few seconds later she laughed—the sound music to Scott's ears. "Well, you always said you wished you could put your life on hold for a while. Now you have. What's that your mom is always saying?"

Scott couldn't help but chuckle. "Be careful what you wish for." The words applied more than she knew.

Just then the door opened, and the small hospital room was filled with shouts and more tears as Scott laughed and cried with his children and his mother, each crowding in for a long-awaited hug.

When his mother straightened from her hug, their eyes remained locked. "What is it, son?" she asked. "Is everything all right?"

Scott remembered his father's parting words. He smiled. His mother's eyes were filled with the joy he'd always remembered being there. "I'll tell you later, Mom."

She patted his hand. "Sure, son. You look tired. We'll talk later."

The children's excessively loud voices and cries had finally reached the ears of Scott's nurse, who poked her head into the room to make sure everything was all right. The shocked expression on her face at seeing Scott conscious brought laughter from the adults as well as the children.

She rushed in and quickly checked his IV and monitor readings, fighting back tears of her own. Clearly she'd grown attached to this small family, and was no doubt happy to see Scott so alert and the children so happy.

Scott asked for some water, which she assured him she would get immediately, just as soon as she paged the doctor. "Merry Christmas," she said just before leaving, giving Kate a knowing wink and then closing the door behind her.

"She's been so good to us, Scott," Kate told him.

Scott's eyes went from Kate to his three children, standing at the side of the bed and all smiles. "I'm sorry I missed Christmas," he told them. "I hope the last four months haven't been too bad for you."

Kate appeared stunned. "How'd you know it's been four months? I . . . haven't told you yet. The doctor suggested waiting until . . ."

Scott smiled at the whispering from his twin girls and the matching shock on the faces of Justin, his own mother, and Kate. "I'll explain *that* a little later as well." His response only deepened the quizzical expressions on three of the five faces.

Meanwhile, his daughters' whisperings had rapidly escalated into bickering. Kate quickly sought to quiet them, but Scott sank his head deeper into his pillow. After all he'd been through, the voices of his children—even bickering—were music to his ears.

It was Caitlin who raised her voice first. "Ashley says we didn't really wait for Daddy because we opened Grandma's Christmas presents."

"Well," shot back Ashley, "we *didn't* wait! I told you he'd wake up, but you—"

"Girls!" Kate put a hand on each of their shoulders and turned to Scott. "All of the kids wanted to hold off opening their gifts until you were awake." She laughed. "I think we're the only family in the world with a Christmas tree up in March."

Justin spoke up next. "I got the lights up, too, Dad. Wait till you see!"

Kate smiled. "They were pretty adamant about making sure you . . . came home for Christmas."

Scott looked at all of them. "It sounds wonderful. Odd, but wonderful." His smile was full and sincere.

"We came and sang you some carols on Christmas Day," Ashley put in next. "Then we went to Grandma's for dinner and to open some presents. But we wanted to open *our* gifts when you could open them with us." Kate gave the girl's shoulder a squeeze. She was beaming. "Wait till you open my gift, Daddy! I know you'll love it!"

"He'll love mine too!" pouted Caitlin.

Scott chuckled again. He felt very weak, but reached out to take Ashley's and then Caitlin's small hands into his own.

His eyes were shining as he looked each of them in the eye, including his mother, his son, and Kate. "All of you . . ." Scott's voice broke before he was able to continue. "All of you are gift enough for me." He smile brightly. "You always will be."

It was a feeling, Scott hoped, that he would never, *ever* forget.

EPILOGUE

Replacing the spool in the lawn trimmer, Scott fed the end of the trimmer line through the small hole and clicked the spool into place as he looked up, catching Justin's eye.

Justin had really stepped up to the plate during Scott's absence, but there was only so much attention to detail found in a twelve-year-old boy. Still, he was immensely proud of him. He'd shoveled snow, keeping the driveway and sidewalk clear all winter, helped out with the twins' homework while keeping up with his own, and had done more than his share of work indoors as well. Kate assured Scott that Justin had been a comfort and a blessing. They both recognized a change in the young man.

Together, the family had decided to clean up the yard a little in preparation for summer. Kate was working in the backyard in her small garden, preparing it for planting later that week. Ashley and Caitlin were in charge of sweeping up the grass clippings from the driveway and sidewalk and raking any other excess grass left behind from the mulching lawn mower. The girls, however, were spending most of their brisk Saturday morning bickering over who could use the push broom as opposed to the regular straw broom. For Scott the whole scene was still satisfying to watch.

He walked out of his garage and started up the trimmer. Justin moved out of the way while Scott trimmed around the first window well. Justin's next job was to lower himself down into the window wells and bag any leaves or trash that had found its way down there. Justin may have matured a great deal since the accident, but Scott still got a kick out of what the boy had chosen to wear for his work attire.

The ends of his jeans were stuffed into calf-length white socks, and a red long-sleeved jacket—a size too small—hugged his body. His hands, each with an oversized work glove on it, gripped a garbage bag and garden rake respectively. His ball cap was turned backward, capping off the outfit, to provide him with what he said was the greatest protection possible from any evil and ferocious spiders that he might happen to disturb. He hadn't complained when given the task, but he had taken what seemed to him the necessary precautions.

He's older, but he's still Justin, thought Scott with a grin.

It was yard work, but it felt good to be doing it—even feeling the burn in his arms and legs as they reluctantly struggled to keep up with all that he had to do.

After waking from his coma, Scott had remained in the hospital for ten days undergoing a series of tests—physical as well as neurological. Thankfully there had been no physical signs of brain damage, which relieved everyone, including himself.

The rest of his body had been a different story. Muscle atrophy, despite the full-range-of-motion exercises he'd been put through during his unconsciousness, had been his biggest hurdle. For the first few days he depended heavily on a walker to get around. After three months of physical therapy, however, he pretty much had full use of his arms and legs, though his right knee still felt a bit stiff from time to time.

Scott found returning to work at the radio station much easier, handling a lot of his business in the beginning over the phone. That didn't go on for very long. Face-to-face communication is what people deserved whenever possible—it was a policy he lived by. He had also, unexpectedly, gained a few more clients as a result of the accident. They'd run across the story of his awakening in the local newspaper. They wanted to work with him, not so much out of pity, but based on the glowing testimonials of existing clients who had been quoted in the article; they'd said that Scott worked hard and never gave up. The message was a powerful one, to small and large businesses alike. Sky, with his Jaguar and big-city ideas, was now leaving him alone, just as Scott had hoped he would. Patience was all that had really been needed to deal with him.

That wasn't to say that Scott's life had become ideal. The tide of medical bills (despite medical and disability insurance) and the recession in general still demanded his concentration if he wished to avoid being sucked into an economic nightmare. But Scott looked at his struggles differently now, satisfied that he was trying to do right and was willing to work hard. As long as he retained these qualities, he knew his family would be blessed—with good or "bad." Both, he now understood, provided blessings from above.

After he had finished trimming around the front of the house, Scott found himself stepping back to take it all in. Each of his family members was working together to make what they had a little nicer. This unity brought to his mind the evening when they'd finally been able to open their Christmas gifts together. Each had been satisfied with the small gifts they'd received, recognizing the fact that a much larger, more valuable gift had already been given them. The kids hadn't complained as Kate and Scott had worried they might while Christmas shopping. And the couple had been grateful for that, hoping that such an attitude would remain with their children for many years to come.

Scott could only hope. He doubted he'd ever forget the message *he'd* been given. He smiled again at the fact that it had been his father who had helped to deliver it—had helped him get back on track.

His mother had simply nodded when Scott had told her all about it. Her only verbal response was, "Well, what do you expect him to do? There are only so many songs you can play on a harp."

Kate had been touched by Scott's vision as well. Tears still came to her eyes every time she thought about it. It had made her feel as if they weren't alone in this life, and that they would never be forgotten.

Scott noticed Kate walking toward him from around the side of the house. She put an arm around him and asked what he was looking at.

"It all looks . . . so nice," he answered. His eyes strayed to each of the children. "All of it."

Kate nodded, seeming to sense what her husband really meant. "It does, doesn't it?" She squeezed him and turned toward him, embracing him in a hug—something they'd been doing a lot lately.

"I couldn't be any happier, Scott. I really couldn't," she said. And then she kissed him.

Scott didn't say anything. He heard the words, as he had so many times before, only this time, he truly believed them.

Author's Note

Elements of doctrine in chapter 21 were taken from *Mormon Doctrine* (Dreams 208, Visions 823–824), *Lectures On Faith* (Lecture Third), 1 Corinthians 10:13, and John 4:14.

ABOUT THE AUTHOR

Jeff graduated from Utah State University with a degree in elementary education, and has been involved in a variety of teaching and mentoring experiences. Currently he teaches junior high in Terreton, Idaho. He is an avid reader who enjoys learning from books as well as people. His first book, *Heaven's Shadow*, was written as a story for his children to enjoy when they are older, and this book follows suit.

Jeff believes strongly in literature that enlightens and edifies. As he puts it: "It was once said of a favorite author of mine, 'Valour and nobility . . . to him must be in every tale for it to be worth the telling.' I strongly believe this to be true, and I'm grateful for those publishers out there striving to produce more uplifting and inspiring material."

Jeff and his wife, Kara, are the parents of four children, and live in Rexburg, Idaho. Jeff enjoys corresponding with his readers, who can write to him in care of Covenant Communications, P.O. Box 416, American Fork, Utah 84003-0416, or e-mail him at info@covenant-lds.com.

Excerpt from

This Just In

by Kerry Blair

Everybody says that a good beginning is the most important part of a book, and I've put a whole lot of thought into this one. I wanted to begin with "It was the best of times, it was the worst of times," because that would sum up my story perfectly, but my editor insists that line has already been taken. Since this is a memoir, my next thought was to begin with "I was born." That too was a no-go. (Can you *believe* the little Dickens took *all* the best openings? What do the rest of us wanna-be writers have to work with—great expectations?)

Never mind. You'll see for yourself why running for my life was the worst—and best—of times for me. And beginning with my birth would have started my story about twenty-five years too early. If this were a movie instead of a book (and I automatically convert all books into movies in my head, don't you?), we'd probably open to a scene of the bustling newsroom hours before someone set out to murder me.

That's me, center screen—Jillanne Caldwell, the perky blond reporter for NewsChannel 2's top-rated morning show, *What's Up, Tucson?* Every weekday between 7 and 9 A.M. I'm out covering everything Arizona has to feature, with "feature" being the operative word. Gila monster races, chili cook-offs, ostrich rodeos—I'm there. Though it's true that I'm never confused with Diane Sawyer, it might be because she doesn't have my flair for fashion and makeup.

If I look familiar to you non-Tucsonans, maybe you saw me in the Miss America pageant a few years back. I was the one who smiled for all she was worth, while the newly crowned Miss America bawled her perfect little eyes out. (There is something backward about that if you ask me, but nobody has.) As first runner-up, I got the in-the-event-Miss-America-is-unable-to-serve lecture, two dozen American Beauty roses, and a "Get into College Free Card." (It beats having *LOSER* written across your forehead in lip liner, but you don't realize it at the time.)

Anyway, if you *have* seen me on TV sampling chili or modeling a swimsuit, you've probably concluded that I'm as fearless as I am beautiful. Conclude again. I would never have gotten myself into those worst/best of times—lost in a desert canyon and being shot at by men who'd give even desperadoes a good name—in order to further my career. (Seriously, bullets aside, do you know what the Sonoran sun can *do* to fair skin?) I went into the wilderness to magnify my calling as a Primary teacher. I went because I love Connor Teagler. I went because, frankly, I'm impetuous and not very bright.

And that, dear reader, brings us to the opening scene of my story.

My first segment of the morning show had just ended and I was back in the newsroom when the report of a lost child came in. Gene, the news director, rushed into the room while I was applying fresh lipstick before I went back out to shoot a special. (The world's largest kiss-in was about to be held at the university and nobody was better qualified to cover it than I was.) Gene waved his arms, scattering interns as he bellowed that a U.S. senator's little kid had gone missing.

I froze in mid-pucker. You don't have to work for CNN to know that there are only two senators from the great state of Arizona, and that one of them hadn't had a child in the house since the Eisenhower administration. Gene must mean Alexander Teagler. I flung my lip brush aside.

It isn't easy to run in high heels, but I'd had enough practice to almost master it. I gained on Gene before he reached the bank of television monitors and lunged for his shirtsleeve.

"Senator Teagler's son?" I gasped. I couldn't stop him, but with my nails stapled to his shirtsleeve, I at least slowed him down a little.

"Tell Dirk to get that helicopter up!" he hollered, dragging me along unnoticed behind him. "Put Kaysie on it."

"No!" I moved my nails from fabric to flesh to get his attention. "Me, Gene! Send *me* with Dirk."

Gene glanced back at last. He seemed genuinely surprised to see a pretty blond feature reporter attached to his arm. He swatted at my hand as if to discourage a mosquito. "This isn't a kiss-in, Jill. It's real news."

"It's Connor!" I said. "Connor Teagler. Isn't it?" My breath came in gasps, but it wasn't from exertion as much as it was fear at the thought of Connor being lost in a place as vast and terrible as the desert mountains north of the city. "He told me his family was going—"

The words brought Gene to a complete halt, so the remainder of my sentence was mumbled into the back of his shirt when I ran into him. He turned and grasped my shoulders. "You *know* Connor Teagler?"

"I'm his Primary teacher," I said. "Last Sunday we were supposed to be learning about how music blesses our lives, but Connor kept interrupting 'If You're Happy and You Know It' to tell us about the trip his family was taking out to their ranch, and . . ." The look on Gene's face told me that not only had "Primary" lost him, but I was also giving altogether too much information. (My propensity for narration is one of my "gifts"—much to the chagrin of everyone who knows me. My mother, who lives with me, tuned me out years ago. My current "boyfriend," who prefers his voice to mine, talks over me. The morning-show producer, who hasn't been able to change me, just cuts me off in mid-word to air commercials.)

I drew a breath to start again with shorter sentences and more pertinent information. "I go to church with Connor's family. I know his mother. She and I went to—"

Gene didn't give me a chance to tell him if Shar and I had gone together to girls' camp or the senior prom. I thought the answer—both—would surprise him, since who would expect a girl who looks like me to have trouble getting a date to prom?

"You *know* Sharon Teagler?" Gene pointed me toward the elevator and propelled me forward until we reached the shiny metal doors. Then he turned me back around to face him. "How *well* do you know her?"

Finally. "We went together to girls' camp and the senior prom."

Gene wasn't surprised. He was delighted. "Do you know where the helipad is?"

"On the roof?" It was a guess—I'd never seen the helicopter up close. Nobody but the pilot and a handful of cameramen and reporters are allowed to set their experienced derrières on its expensive seats. Still, it was an *educated* guess, since you can't exactly park a chopper in the basement next to the news vans.

Gene pushed me backward through the now-open elevator doors, but he didn't release his hold on my shoulders. I hoped his hands weren't sweating as much as his forehead, because perspiration is murder to get out of a raw silk-blouse.

"This thing'll go national," he said. With his eyes raised to heaven it seemed as if he were telling God rather than me. He muttered a few more things I hope God missed, and pulled me back out of the elevator. "I can't send Reporter Barbie to cover something this big."

I stiffened. It's not exactly a secret that the prettier one's face, the "fluffier" her assignments, but I *am* a reporter, darn it. So what if my tuition was paid by a scholarship from the Miss America Corporation? I graduated from the Walter Cronkite School of Journalism at Arizona State University with a diploma as valid as anybody else's. And so what if the most investigative reporting I'd done thus far involved detecting Slim Fast on the breath of a blue-ribbon greyhound? I'm willing to work my way to the top of my profession one dog-and-pony show at a time. Even Walter Cronkite couldn't become poster boy of the Fourth Estate overnight. And Mr. Cronkite had a few advantages: for one, he never had to wax off his mustache; for another, it didn't take him half an hour between assignments to fix his makeup. (On the other hand, *he* never looked as good on TV as I do. It was lucky for Walter that television was black and white when he started out.)

But even apart from my qualifications as a journalist, I had to convince Gene to let me go. So I did what I always do when my toes start to curl and I feel an anxiety attack coming on—I prayed. When you've prayed as many different prayers in as many different places and under as many different circumstances as I have, you get to where you can do it fast and fervently at the same time. Sometimes it's just one word—*please*. This time the word was *Connor*.

All history with his mother aside, I loved Connor Teagler more than anything. He was one of the only real things in my Barbie Dream House life. I stood outside that elevator and choked back tears as I remembered the first day Connor sat next to me in Primary. He'd stroked my long, lacquered nails with his chubby little fingers and asked, "Are they real?"

"Real acrylic," I admitted.

The next week he had asked about my highlighted hair, thick eyelashes, and full lips. He might have proceeded farther down if I hadn't clutched the lesson manual over my chest and steered the conversation back to Jesus wanting him for a Sunbeam. Week after week, Connor was full of questions, surprises, and surprising insight. I'd sit in the classroom after Primary thinking that if I could become as *this* little child, maybe I could figure out, at last, why a girl who apparently had everything wanted something else.

But today Connor was missing, and whether it made sense or not, I somehow felt it was up to me to find him. The first step to following that spiritual prompting was to get through Gene onto that helicopter.

My smile is often called "perky," which would not get me what I wanted at the moment, so it was good that the face I raised to my boss was unhappy. I straightened the front pleats in my designer skirt and wished it were an inch or two longer and that my tousled hair was upswept instead. I would have to rely on my manner to convey dignity and competence.

"Shar Teagler will talk to me," I told Gene firmly. "She won't talk to another reporter."

It was a bold statement, considering the fact that Shar had barely spoken to me since her wedding day. I hadn't seen her, in fact, until serendipity—and a lucrative modeling contract—put us both back in the same ward. (At least for the months she and her senator husband spent in Arizona.)

I thought when I first saw her at church that our reunion would be something like the one in *Beaches*, but the reality was more like *Ice Age*. After being frozen out of Shar's social circle at one ward social, two Enrichment Nights, and a Primary Activity Day, I finally (if resentfully) accepted my new role in her life. I no longer co-starred as the best friend of the young, impeccably styled wife of Arizona's fastest-rising political star. I had been recast as an extra—the Primary teacher whose one minor scene ends up on the cutting-room floor.

That whole movie-as-life-metaphor was the way Shar and I had coped with our poverty-stricken adolescence. The year we turned eleven—old enough to command the respect of infants and young children—we founded KidSitters in the housing project where we lived. For the next seven years we invested every dime we earned babysitting in the nearby dollar theater. On Wednesdays, dollar movies showed for fifty cents, which was within even our limited budgets. If a flick was worth seeing, we saw it. If it was really worth seeing (meaning Val Kilmer or Chris O'Donnell or somebody equally attractive was in it) we saw it twice. Or thrice. Or . . . you get the idea. When we weren't sitting in the theater, we were waiting to be discovered by boys and cast in glamorous starring roles in romances of our own.

All things considered, it was an idyllic life. With Shar at my side, I didn't notice that my father was gone and my mother was depressed. (Although it did occur to me that Mom took too many pills and lost too many jobs.) Shar and I were inseparable. At least we were until we did what too many best friends do—we grew up and let a man come between us.

Six years later, I looked Gene square in the eye and repeated, "Shar will talk to me." After all, it *might* be true. Maybe this *was* the day Shar would put the bad part of our past—the part where she'd met and married Alex Teagler—behind her and remember instead all the really great years that had gone before.

Gene looked at me as if he were standing before an all-you-can-eat buffet that displayed nothing but raw squid, chopped liver, and chicken gizzards. At last he closed his eyes and released the delicate fabric of my blouse. "Go, Jillanne," he said, pushing the "roof" button in the elevator. "Don't come back without a Pulitzer."

Thankfully, neither of us knew then that I almost wouldn't come back at all.

A Personal Note from Jill: Surprise! You probably picked up this book thinking you were getting a great adventure story—and you are!—but little did you dream you'd also get fantabulous tips garnered from my years of experience with fellow pageant contestants, professional makeup artists, and extensive perusal of just about every fashion magazine printed in the English language. (Plus some things I thought of as I went along and just had to throw in!) I hope you like the idea because, frankly, my editor isn't sold on it. She's worried that guys will see my "advice columns," decide this is a chick book, and toss it aside. But I know better. I mean, you men are smart enough to just turn the page and get on with the drama, right? I knew it! All my male readers may now be excused to go on to Chapter 2. Meanwhile, ladies, you're in for a treat!

Jill's Tips for Luscious Lips

Even when you have every intention of keeping your lips to yourself, you want them to look luscious enough to kiss. Here are some tricks of the trade:

Like me, you probably know women who swear by a certain expensive brand of lipstick, but I say the lipstick itself isn't nearly as important as the way you use it. I buy my lipstick at the corner drugstore because I figure why pay $30 or more for one lousy shade when you can get ten lipsticks for the same price and mix them together to create colors that are uniquely your own? To do this, put tiny portions of two or more sticks into each compartment of a small, plastic pillbox. Pop it in the microwave for just a few seconds and then mix with a toothpick. Voila! Now you have seven colors nobody else can buy. They not only look great, they're easy to take anywhere!

The style now is to skip lip liner, but this won't work if you have a blurry lip line, thin lips, or if you have dark hair and fair skin and don't want your lips to seem to disappear. To provide definition, use a pencil to apply the liner first in a thick line, making it wide on the sides of the lips, particularly the bottom lip. Then blend the inside edges into your lips with a dry brush and apply the lipstick, keeping it only on the center where there is no liner. Blend well. (I learned this from the girl who placed third at the Miss America pageant. It's guaranteed to make your lips look shapely instead of flat like hers.)

A couple more things you should know: to make your teeth look really white, mix up a lipstick in a blue/red or wine/plum. Shades with too much brown can make even white teeth look dingy. Use different lipsticks to add the illusion of fullness. (This is why you buy cheap and get more.) Apply the darker base to your lips, and then use a little light lipstick on the bottom center. You can also use light lipstick in the lower center of your top lip (near the bow) to make your lips look larger and fuller.

Does this sound complicated for something that will only last a few hours at best? It is! But makeup is an illusion, and nobody ever said magic—or glamour—is easy. If you're on your way to the store or to school, I say gloss and go. But for a photo, a special night out, or those once-in-a-lifetime pageants and kiss-ins, luscious is a look you'll like!

Excerpt from

This Just In

CHAPTER 2

Come to find out, I hate helicopters.

Sure, they get you up in the air fast, but this is not an advantage when you're a girl who's lost more than one partially digested corn dog on a Ferris wheel. And while they cover a remarkable amount of ground in remarkably little time, you can't actually *see* any of it. (Unless the blur I saw was just my life passing before my eyes.) But the worst thing about them has got to be the *transparency* of the things. I felt like Glinda the Good Witch of the North, except my bubble didn't float tranquilly over a yellow-brick road. It bobbed wildly around skyscrapers and satellite antennas before roaring out over the freeway.

I probably screamed, but there was no way to know for sure, since I went deaf about the time the pilot started the engine. I thought I might have gone blind, too, but then I realized I just hadn't opened my eyes since the moment we'd almost creamed that poor, myopic pigeon.

When Dirk Hadden, NewsChannel 2's Guy in the Sky, tossed a combination headphone-mic into my lap, I finally opened my eyes to regard him dumbly. Then I looked down at the gizmo and wondered how much it would cost me to replace the piece of equipment when I slimed it with the thick goo that churned in my stomach and rose to my throat. (Of all the times to leave behind my tranquilizers, this was the worst.)

"Put them on," Dirk mouthed through the roar of the chopper.

And let go of these metal bars? Not likely. Clearly, my contribution—clutching the underbars of my seat and pulling upward with all my strength—was the only thing keeping us airborne. If I let go we would spiral out of control like an overgrown dragonfly and splatter across the windshields of who-knew-how-many semis on the inter-state below.

"Put them on," he shouted. "You'll need to hear this."

I ignored him. I knew I wouldn't be able to hear over the pounding of my heart anyway. But when Dirk released the control stick to reach for the headphones himself, I reconsidered. One of my white-knuckled hands shot up and plunked the headset over my ears (careless, for once, of my hairstyle) before returning to its death-grip on my seat.

"Having fun, Babe?" Dirk asked, guffawing at his own warped sense of humor. He pulled the chopper into a wide arc that left my stomach heading north for Phoenix while the rest of me veered east toward the open desert.

Silently calling Dirk a jerk—and a few other nice-girl expletives—I gaped at the mountains. At this distance the Galiuros still looked blue and purple. With ragged peaks jutting into the blue, near-autumn sky, they looked incredible. But while they made a great postcard picture, they were the worst place imaginable for a little boy to be lost.

A native of the area, I had heard enough history to know that for the better part of a century, bands of renegade Apaches led by men whose names had passed into history—Victorio, Cochise, and Geronimo—had used these mountains to elude cavalry forces that often outnumbered them more than a hundred to one. Bravely, stub-bornly, savagely they held on to what little they had, often relying on a labyrinth of hidden caverns to conceal themselves from their enemies, and sparse desert vegetation to sustain their lives. Even the hardiest men raised in these mountains struggled to stay alive in them. How could a frightened little boy who grew up in a mansion possibly survive out there for more than a few hours . . . especially all alone?

The fresh wave of fear was pushed from my mind as a familiar voice came over the headphones. Gene gave Dirk instructions and then told me to listen carefully to an upcoming feed from the reporter already on location. Senator Teagler was about to make a statement.

Dirk gunned the engine as though he thought he might be able to get the chopper down before the senator said his first word. I closed my eyes again. I had no doubt we'd make it back to the ground—I just didn't believe it would be in fewer pieces than the average jigsaw puzzle. My hair began to turn gray one silky blond strand at a time.

Then it hit me.

"There's a reporter there already?" I managed to squeak around the lump in my throat. (The goo had hardened into cement.) *How did somebody get there before us?* I wanted to ask. *And why couldn't I ride with him instead of you?*

"There's a slew of reporters on-ground," Dirk responded. "Teagler had a press conference scheduled before his kid disappeared this morning."

"Huh?"

Dirk laughed, again. (And it wasn't *with* me, if you know what I mean.) "Don't catch much news, do you, Babe?" he said. "This is the day Alexander Teagler was set to announce his primary candidacy."

Primary candy see? I didn't see at all. His words made no sense. (It's very hard to think rationally when you're bouncing around in a plastic bubble, two minutes and five hundred feet away from a particularly unattractive death.)

"He's running for president of the United States," Dirk said. It didn't escape my attention that he said it in the same tone of voice I use to talk to Sunbeams.

"And he's announcing it in the desert because he wants the rattlesnakes to be the first to know?" I asked, forgetting for the moment the significance of Alex standing on the front porch of his ancestral estate.

I have a bad habit of speaking before I think. One of my former boyfriends used to say it's because I'm blond, but I seriously doubt it has all that much to do with my hair color, as almost-natural as it is. As soon as I heard my own dumb question, I knew the answer. Teagler's ancestors were among the original settlers of the area, unless you include the American Indians. When you add the Apache and Tohono O'odam to the equation, the Teaglers were several thousand years too late to add "original" to their title of "settler." While most Tucsonans living in the 1800s huddled within the relative safety of the town and relied on General Crook, et al, to preserve and protect their "right" to the Indians' ancestral land, the Teagler family staked out a sizeable ranch on the best bottomland and spent generations fighting hostile Apaches to keep it. (At least, that was how I'd always heard the story.) Anyway, since Alex Teagler had begun his political career in Tucson, it was probably obvious to everybody else in the nation why he'd returned home today to announce the furtherance of it.

In the next moment, the headphones over my ears filled with static, followed by Alex's rich, sonorous voice. Even though his only child was missing, his voice didn't waver. He was a born public speaker. Heck, he was a born politician. Alexander Teagler had it all—big smile, big hair, big head, and only a passing familiarity with the meaning of integrity.

I listened as Alex thanked the local dignitaries, the press, and the search-and-rescue teams for being there. (It sounded like he was addressing the last session of a stake conference. I almost expected him to add, "Now, be courteous as you're out there looking for my son. We don't want any accidents on the way home.") Then he said regretfully that, although there had been another reason for asking the media to come, their presence was providential in that it afforded him the opportunity to ask the nation to join him in prayer for the safe return of his little boy. He referred to the picture of Connor that he was holding and said what a joy he was. At that point, his voice broke. Finally, he explained that he was appearing alone because his wife had locked herself inside the ranch house, distraught over Connor's disappearance because she felt it was her fault.

"My wife is young," Alex explained to the press corps. "And inexperienced. I blame myself for not bringing our au pair along with us last night."

It was clear to me—though knowing his luck, it probably wasn't to the million other people listening in on headphones, radios, and televisions all over America—that Teagler didn't blame himself at all. He blamed Shar.

I let go of the seat and clutched my plastic-encased ears instead. "Did he say—?"

Dirk cut me off with a wave of his hand and pointed to his own head-piece to show me he still wanted to listen to the senator even if I didn't.

Suddenly, the helicopter couldn't move fast enough to suit me. I needed to find that little boy and take him back to my best friend.

(As crazy as it sounds, at that moment I not only felt I *should* find Connor, I believed I *would*.)

Before I could tap my little red three-inch heels together thrice, my wish was granted. We swooped down toward the sprawling ranch just as I was about to start muttering, "There's no place like home." Almost falling off the seat brought me back to reality.

There were at least six helicopters and two light planes already on the ground or circling the area. I recognized a few of them from other news stations in Tucson and Phoenix, but the rest were law enforcement, search-and-rescue, and—my heart skipped a beat—MedEvac. I closed my eyes and told myself that the latter was only a precaution. They'd never need it. After all, the long, circular drive already flickered with red, blue, and yellow strobes from emergency vehicles. Already, hundreds of people had arrived to search for Connor Teagler. He'd be safe before sunset. He had to be.

"I'll set you down there," Dirk said, heading toward a recently vacated spot on the ground. "I'll be around, but catch a ride back to town with one of the ground crew, would you?" He tossed a small station bag into my lap. I knew it contained a radio, tape recorder, and other tools of the trade, but I didn't catch it. My hands were once again glued to the bars under my seat. Petrified, I watched it fall between my shaking knees and onto the floor at my feet. I left it where it lay.

A new voice snickered in my headphones. It was Art, the cameraman wedged into the small area behind the seats. He was already at work, feeding live panoramic views to the studio anchors that had undoubtedly interrupted the soaps with the more-dramatic news of a lost child. I hoped all those viewers wouldn't agree with Alex's implication that Shar had been negligent, but I hoped they would take in the view of the miles and miles of barren desert and remember to pray for Connor.

The helicopter took a dip more sudden than a runaway elevator, but still I managed to turn my scream of terror into one of protest. "Wait! I don't want to be put down!" I told Dirk. I could scarcely believe the words myself—I definitely didn't relish staying aboard this roaring bubble of doom. But I heard myself continue, "I want to help look for Connor."

Despite his lack of good sense and common decency, Dirk might well be the best pilot in the business. A Marine reservist, he's fearless, tireless, and willing to play a hunch. Since news stations afford them more eyes in the sky, law enforcement agencies are generally tolerant of news-chopper jockeys, but they *like* Dirk. He stays professional, stays on top of the scanner, and is willing to take the risks. More often than not, he's the guy (in the sky) who gets the job done. I knew staying with him might be my best chance of finding Connor.

"Take me with you!" I pleaded.

"No can do, Babe," he said affably. His grin told me he had taken the mechanical bug down faster than was technically necessary, just for the thrill of seeing my face fade from parchment-colored to paste to bleached bone. "Your job is to make nice with the kid's family. Mine is to find the kid."

I felt the helicopter's landing gear—or whatever you call those parallel strips of flimsy aluminum—scrape into the desert floor as if into my spine. The copter shuddered to a stop, but the blades at the top of the craft kept whirring.

No wonder they call them choppers, I thought. *It's like sitting beneath the spinning knives of a giant food processor.* I shrank down in my seat.

"Duck on your way out," Dirk advised.

"Aren't you going to turn it *off?*" I gasped.

Dirk's grin widened as he shook his head.

Sadist.

From behind my seat, Art reached forward and opened the escape hatch. Then he undid my harness.

I leaned tentatively out the door to look up at the chopper blades. I decided they were probably too high to lop too much off my recently styled do. Then I looked down at the ground and wondered if it would be unprofessional to kiss the terra firma once I'd fallen down there on my knees and all.

Dirk retrieved the station bag from the floor and looped one of its straps over my head. Then he started to reach for my headphones, but paused at the sight of another chopper coming down nearby. I heard his low whistle through the earpiece. "They brought in the top gun," he told Art, motioning toward the new helicopter.

The craft was still more than a hundred feet in the air, but the side door had opened and a pair of long, jean-encased legs swung over the side as it continued to descend. I held my breath as an athletic man with dark hair grasped a slender line with one hand and dropped to the ground. Landing agilely, he pulled the strap of a leather bag more securely over his broad shoulders and sprinted toward a long white van with the words "Pinal County Mobile Command Center" printed prominently on its side.

"Who's that?" I asked. Except for the lack of cape and cowl, I figured it might be Batman. (Or at least a darker, better-looking version of Val Kilmer.)

"That's Clay Eskiminzin," Dirk said through my earphones. "Steer clear of him."

"Why?"

"He hates reporters," Art supplied. I wanted to ask why he hated journalists. I wanted to know why Dirk called him "the top gun." Most of all, I wanted to find Connor and go back home—slowly and by land vehicle. But meanwhile, as shallow as it sounds to come right out and admit it, I really wanted to meet Batguy up close and personal. Unfortunately, I wasn't given enough time to come up with a plan.

"So long, Babe." Dirk pulled off my headphones as he pushed me from the helicopter. "Good luck. You're gonna need it."

He was right about that last thing.